William Hurrell Mallock

A Romance of the Nineteenth Century

Vol. 1

William Hurrell Mallock

A Romance of the Nineteenth Century
Vol. 1

ISBN/EAN: 9783337346805

Printed in Europe, USA, Canada, Australia, Japan

Cover: Foto ©Andreas Hilbeck / pixelio.de

More available books at **www.hansebooks.com**

of the

NINETEENTH CENTURY

BY

W. H. MALLOCK

AUTHOR OF 'THE NEW REPUBLIC' ETC.

'DEFECERUNT OCULI MEI IN SALUTARE TUUM'

IN TWO VOLUMES—VOL. I.

London

CHATTO AND WINDUS, PICCADILLY

1881

LONDON : PRINTED BY
SPOTTISWOODE AND CO., NEW-STREET SQUARE
AND PARLIAMENT STREET

CHAPTER I.

THE talents, the family, and the fortune of Ralph Vernon were all quite distinguished enough to make it worth the world's while to attend to him; and the result was that he was at once condemned and courted. This was not perhaps a matter that it is very hard to account for. His manners and his amusements led him to consort with the careless, whilst his deeper interests were really those of the serious; and thus, let him be in what society he would, he was always in a moral sense more or less an

outsider. He had little of the gay good-
fellowship which is the virtue most prized by
the pleasure-seekers ; he was on the surface
far too much of a pleasure-seeker not to
irritate those who are busied with thoughts
of duty : and his faults, actual or imputed,
when they came to the general ear, repelled
the one class without attracting the other.

It was supposed that he had trifled with
the affections of numerous women ; it was
supposed that he had wasted any amount of
talent ; it was supposed that, from knowledge
or want of knowledge, he was without any
kind of Christianity, and that, from want of
earnestness, he was quite unmoved by its
substitutes ; he was supposed to have many
friends warmly attached to him, and to be
himself incapable of any warm attachment.
And this marked want in him of all that is
thought most lovable was made more marked
still by his singular charm of manner, which,

for the time being, was certain to win every
one. Such was the general impression of
him, which, whether true or no, was at all
events not groundless ; and there was many
a mother in London of the best and purest
type who thought his character so cold, so
unprincipled, and so repulsive, that he could
atone for it only by becoming her daughter's
husband.

The number of these mothers was at last
reduced to one. Ralph Vernon became engaged to be married. The *fiancée* was young,
clever, beautiful, and deeply attached to him ;
nor in the case of most men would the event
have seemed unnatural. But the general
sentiment with regard to Vernon was merely
wonder as to what could be here his motive :
for most of the world thought what a rough-
tongued cousin of his said, 'You may see me
d—d if Ralph's ever in love with any one.'
Let his motive, however, be what it might,

his engagement caused, or was caused by, a
very visible change in him.   All of a sudden
he seemed to become serious ; and for many
months one might have thought him a new
man.   The father of the bride-elect was at
the time absent in Afghanistan, and the
marriage was put off till his return the following year.   Vernon, meanwhile, said good-bye
to his idleness ; he was even not liberal in
the days he allowed for love-making.   He
devoted himself instead to his various county
duties ; he studied such subjects as education
and pauperism ; he projected the building of
schools and cottages ; and he tried to become
acquainted with the great mass of his
tenantry.   Finally, when in 1880, came the
renowned general election, he stood in the
Conservative interest for his own division of
the county, and lost the battle by less than
a dozen votes.

This sudden devotion to public affairs,

however, was not construed altogether to his advantage. It was supposed to argue luke-warmness in love, rather than zeal in politics ; nor was the rumour at all wondered at that the lady took the same view of it. Vernon, it was said on all sides, was not behaving well ; it was added by many that he wished to back out of his engagement; and the latter opinion was certainly confirmed by the sequel. In due time the lady's father returned, and the various legal preliminaries were at once to be got over. What, then, were the feelings of all who heard it when Vernon insisted, as one condition of his marriage, that any children that might result from it should be brought up as Catholics ! The father and the family of the *fiancée* were all fiercely Protestant; and this move of Vernon's made an end of the whole matter. The rupture was abrupt and painful ; and he was himself severely criticised. That he had

any interest in religion was what nobody
gave him credit for ; and he was supposed,
in this case, to have used it as a last excuse
in his desperation.

His conduct directly afterwards did not
disarm the censorious. He was soon reported
to have formed another intimacy, and to
have given another lady a strong sentimental
claim on him. Then, the report went on,
he had repeated his former conduct, though
this time perhaps more judiciously. There
had been no formal engagement, the world
supposed ; there had been no need, therefore,
for any definite subterfuge. A simpler ex-
pedient had been quite sufficient : he had
buried himself somewhere in some retreat on
the Continent. This second drama had been
of a strictly private character ; but there are
acute observers who can pierce through any
privacy ; and the comments made on it were
not of a friendly nature. Indeed, when the

news was known that after all his mis-
demeanours Vernon was enjoying himself in
a charming Provençal villa, surrounded by
books, and supplied with a first-class *chef*, one
of the keenest and most discriminating of all
his feminine acquaintances was at last tempted
to speak of him as a voluptuary of the very
worst species.

In spite, however, of every ill report,
there were a certain number who always
stood up for him, and who maintained stoutly
that there were two sides to his character.
They could not deny that what the world
said was true of him ; they declared only
that it was not the whole truth. There was
one of these in especial—Alic Campbell
by name—who looked upon Vernon as the
best friend he had, and who knew much of
his inner history that was quite hidden from
others. When Vernon went abroad, he had
begged Campbell to go with him ; but

Campbell for certain reasons had felt constrained to refuse. Vernon had written from
Paris to him, to renew his entreaties, but
without the desired result. About a fortnight later he returned to the charge once
more.

CHAPTER II.

'MY dear Alic,' he wrote, 'I am at last settled; and I will now take no denial. You must and you shall join me. Could you only see where I am, I should have no need to implore you; you would come instantly, and come of your own accord. As it is, I can only trust to writing; but you surely will not refuse me. Come to me do, if for no more than a week or two, and share with me this beautiful Southern solitude. Share my villa with its cool portico—a villa just large enough for two children of Epicurus. Share my

garden with its myrtles, and its oranges, and
the softly swaying gold of its great mimosa-
trees. Yes, I am here in the South and the
clear sunshine ; and I am not, as you pro-
phesied and as half my heart urged me, in
any of the winter haunts of English fashion
and frivolity; but I am embowered safely by
myself on the greenest of all the promontories
that Europe juts into the Mediterranean. I
am settled at the Cap de Juan. I have,
indeed, chosen a lovely spot, and already I
love it tenderly. All day long, through the
leaves of my dark evergreens, and through
arched bowery openings, the sea shines and
sparkles. You and I may change and grow
weary ; and we have both had much to weary
us. But this bluest of blue seas seems to be
always one-and-twenty; and as I breathe its
breath, full of eternal freshness, the thrill and
the dreams of youth once more revive in me.
And ah, the view! In a vast majestic

crescent the French coast of mountains curves away towards Italy, with its succession of pearl-grey headlands dying faintly and far off into the distance. Midway, about ten miles from here as a boat sails, a line of milk-white houses, Nice lies along the sea-level. Range upon range is piled up behind it, blue with far-off haze, or green with nearer olive-woods ; and bright over all, like the hills of another world, are the jagged Alpine summits with their white snows glittering. All day long the lights and the tints vary. New mists form and melt upon the mountains ; the sea changes from one glow to another. The wave-worn sea-rock, pierced with its clear shadows, has always new hues and aspects ; so have the silver gleams that sleep in the spreading stone-pines. The whole face of Nature is like the face of a living thing. It is the face of a Cleopatra.

> Age cannot wither it, nor custom stale
> Its infinite variety.

'Alic—you who are coughing, sneezing, and blowing your nose in England—will not this tempt you? Your first impulse will be, I know, to refuse me. You are not in spirits, you will say, for the sunshine; you have no energy left to make any exertion. I am quite familiar with the mood of mind you are in. You are like a man who is sea-sick at the extreme end of a steamer, and who yet will not move himself to make his way to the middle. You are arguing to yourself with the unique logic of grief, " I am comfortless, and therefore nothing shall comfort me." Let me try to move you to a brighter and a healthier mind.

'You are wretched, you tell me, because you want to marry a certain person, and because you find that, though she loves you as a friend, she will never love you but as a friend only. Now, I am going to speak very gently to you, and yet I hope convincingly.

I am not going to tell you any such idle lies
as that your loss is a trifling one. I am not
going to tell you that it is an atom less than
you feel it to be; and you would, I think,
injure your character by trying to undervalue
it. No; I will not tell you to undervalue
your loss. I will only show you—a thing
you have quite forgotten—how to value your
gain. Perhaps you will say I am not in a
position to do so, for in some ways certainly
you have been somewhat reticent. You have
told me much about your own feelings, about
your own devotion, and about the moral result that all this has had on you. But about
the object of these feelings you have told me
little. I know neither how you met her nor
how you wooed her ; nor anything about her
character, except that her ways are simple.
You have not told me even her name. But
I don't think this matters. Let the difference
between our two situations be what it may,

your case in many ways has been also mine ;
and I am going now to speak from my own
experience.

' I, as you know well, was not long since
to have married ; and during a good year's
novitiate I was preparing my whole being for
its solemn new condition. My character
during that period underwent a profound
change. My bright-coloured hopes and purposes lost their airy wings. They fell to the
solid earth, and found for themselves plodding
feet. I felt I was no longer my own. My
life was owed to another ; and for the first
time there dawned on me the true sense of
responsibility. But circumstances combined
to make my marriage impossible ; and after
I had already learned to mentally mix my life
with another's, our two lives were again made
separate. When first I realised this, it was
like waking out of a dream. I was conscious
of a loneliness I had never known before ;

and even now, with my shattered marriage prospects, my manhood seems to lie in ashes about me. But what do I find has happened? Something glad, strange, and altogether un-looked for. Out of the ashes of my manhood has re-arisen my youth—my youth, which I thought I had said good-bye to for eternity; and the divine child has again run to meet me with its eyes bright as ever, and with the summer wind in its hair. The sun has gone back for me on the dial. I am three years younger again. The skies seem to have grown bluer, and my step more elastic. Once more free and unfettered, I feel sometimes as if I were walking on air; and I have the delicious sense of having lost a burden, even though I may have lost a treasure as well.

'You will see my meaning better when I go on to tell you that, though I have re-covered the buoyancy of youth, I have by no means recovered its ignorance. I still retain

a certain salvage of wisdom, sad and bitter
enough in some ways, and yet good for men
like us two to remember. It is this—listen
patiently. There is nothing in the world so
intensely selfish as a woman's deep affection ;
and the stronger and more single-hearted it
is, the greater becomes its selfishness. A
man's passion is generous when compared
with a woman's love. A man's passion, at
its worst, lasts but a short time ; even while
it lasts, its demands are limited ; and, what is
more than this, a good man will restrain it.
But the truer and more sensitive a woman is,
the more thoroughly will she let her love
master her ; the less effort will she make to
retain the least control of it.

'And what a master it is ! Its jealousy
is cruel as the grave, and its demands know
no limits but the imagination of her that
makes them. A woman who loves thus is
not content with the chastest bodily con-

stancy; she is not content even with the constancy of an undivided tenderness. These she takes for granted: they are not the things she craves for. What she craves for is the constancy of your whole thought and intellect. You are to have nothing in your mind that you do not confide to her; you are to stifle every interest with which she cannot be associated. If you want any mental help, it is she alone who must help you; and she had sooner you were helped ill by her than well by another person. She will be as jealous of your friendships as she is of your affections, and as jealous of your thoughts and tastes as she is of your friendships. She cannot patiently conceive of you as in relation to anything excepting herself. She desires to absorb your whole life into hers; and the larger part of it, which she naturally cannot absorb, she desires to see perish. Her pleading, earnest eyes will be for ever saying

to you, " Entreat me not to leave thee.
Where thou goest I will go ; and go not thou,
my love, whither I cannot follow thee."

'What!—with all the world of thought
and imagination before us, are men such as
we are to be tied and bound like this ? For
my part, the wings of my spirit seem to have
all the winds in them ; and I have a heart
sometimes likes a hawk's or a wild sea-gull's.
It is not a heart that is hard, or that does
not soften to companionship. I could often
perch tenderly upon some beloved shoulder,
and bend my head to listen to words of
tenderness. But if the hand that I trusted
but once closed to lay hold of me—dared,
from love, to use the least pressure to keep
me—I should start and struggle, and feel I
had suffered treachery. I will stoop my
neck myself; but no one else shall ever draw
it an inch downwards. Why do we want
companionship ? What is a man's need for it ?

Were my life really a bird's, I would gladly have a she-bird to fly with me ; but I would have her only because we were bound both of us independently for the same resting-place. That and that alone should be the fetterless fetter we were united by. But a woman who loves deeply will never love like this. She has no wish to be your companion on these terms. It is not the common end that she cares for, but the united struggle ; and she reveres her wish to soar, chiefly because it is an excuse for clinging to you. Thus, on the same principle, she will go nowhere in the mental world herself unless you are there to support her. She thinks it a kind of treason to you to try and walk independently. She cultivates her weakness, that she may be always trusting to your strength ; and though her weight might be dragging you to the ground, she would never think of it, never see it, but if possible she would only lean the heavier. Was ever selfishness so pitiless and intense as this ? And yet, by a strange magic, it looks so like self-devotion, that a man, if he be not a brute, can hardly fail to be crushed by it. Such love, Alic, may be a thing that suits some temperaments, but surely neither yours nor mine.

'And now I am once more my own. Ah, the sweetness and rest of this serene self-possession! But lately I felt, when I was looking even at the sea or the mountains, that I was not permitted to love them. The shadow of another would always seem to cleave to me and claim me ; and I could no longer let my spirit, as I used to do, go floating on the lonely waters. But now I can look everywhere without fear. I can say to the sea, when it makes me in love with loneliness, " I violate no allegiance due to any companionship." I can say the same to the forest, when its leafy smells woo me, and

the murmur of its brown branches. I can
say the same in society, when bright eyes
and alluring voices stimulate me, and I feel
that many women are far better than one.
Then, too—though I will not dwell upon this
here—were there a God to turn to, I could
turn to Him in solitude. And now in the
morning, as I awaken, I often turn to my
pillow, and kiss it, and say, "No head but
mine can ever dare to press you." All the
walls of my bedroom seem to smile kindly
and quietly on me. By my bedside I see my
dear companions, my books—so varied and
so unobtrusive—that will themselves tell me
all they can, and will ask for no confidence in
return; and there, too, I see my letters,
which have now the new charm for me, that
no one but myself will ever want to open
them.

'Yes; I have learned the truest secret of
Epicurus, that the friendship of a man is

more than the love of a woman. Friendship
is always a free gift ; and it is always given
readily because it is never owed. Love, too,
begins as a gift ; but a loving woman will
never leave it so. Before you know it, she
will have turned it into a debt; and the
more she loves the debtor, the more oppres-
sively will she extort the utmost farthing
from him. But between friends, Alic, the
intercourse is always free. I could have no
thought that it would be treason to conceal
from you. I could form no ties or friendships that would do you any wrong. And
yet—if I may alter Shakespeare in a single
word—

> And yet, by heaven, I hold my *friend* as rare
> As any she belied by false compare.

'Come, then, and lay all this to your
heart ; for your heart, I know, will assent to
its truth as mine does. Marriage would suit
you no better than me. It allured me first

with its many pleasing promises ; and in the same way it is now alluring you. It can give much to numbers ; I do not deny that for a moment ; but neither you nor I were made for it. In missing it, as I have said before, you are no doubt a loser ; but my advice to you is, do not brood over the loss ; think of the gain, for the gain is far greater. Recall your imagination from the solace you would have had in marriage, and dwell on the joys and the freedom that you keep because you are single.

' Freedom—yes, you have that still. You have not the caprices of any one else to bind you. My dear Alic, think of your priceless freedom ! I say think of it ; but I want you to use it also. I want you to come to me, away from your frosty England, and let me see the Southern sunlight laughing in your glad grey eyes. If you will, all my house shall welcome you. My champagne is excellent ;

my cigars and cigarettes are excellent—I had
them all sent from London ; and my bookcases
are well stored with poets, and with your own
philosophers. At the end of one of my walks
is a certain marble seat. You look straight
down at the sea from it, and it is overarched
with myrtles. There is a perfect wilderness
of green shade behind it ; and in the midst of
this, like an enchanted lamp, is a great
camellia tree, burning with scarlet blossoms.
Close at hand there is a little table, just fit to
support a bottle of Burgundy, and a quaint
old glass goblet for each of us. It is an
entrancing place. It is a bower after your
own heart. And there we might sit together,
in the calm, delicious mornings, talking or
silent, just as the mood prompted us. Sometimes we might quote to each other our
favourite poets ; sometimes we might solve
again the old insoluble questions we have so
often discussed before, and which are still

eating my life out; sometimes we might watch in quiet the waves and the rocks before us, and often, too, some gay, bright-coloured fishing-boat, floating lonely with its white plume of a sail, and its brown fisher at the stern bending over his own reflection. Yes, Alic, if you will only come out to me, we will contrive to elude the Furies. We will look into life together more clearly than we used to do; but it shall be a personal oppression to us no more than it used to be. We will only enter here on a new phase of youth. We will have free, cloudless days, and nights of moonlight. We will drive, and ride, and sail, and explore the whole country. We will know the folds of the hills grey with olive-trees; we will listen to the sound of mule-bells; we will see how the middle-age lingers in the wild hill-villages. Then, too, my own immediate neighbourhood—that is delightful also. The whole of my green peninsula is an

Eden of woods and gardens ; and the life
that surrounds you there is like a living idyll.
Old brown crones crouching under the olive-
trees, the peasant proprietor tilling his small
field, the neatly dressed nursery-gardener
surveying his glass frames, the retired
domestic tradesman smiling over the gate of
his little villa-garden—these are the living
images that surround one, and that give to
one's thoughts such a quaint, delightful setting. A strange mixture, too, on all sides
touches one of homely plenty and of wild
luxuriance. Cabbages and palm-trees grow
in the same enclosure. Between beds of
kitchen stuff are strips starred with anemones,
and pink almond-blossoms tremble among the
apple-trees.

'Ah, my old companion, will not these
pleasures move you ? Write, write to me
quickly, and say they will. Only in that case
I have something further to tell you. If you

would enjoy the seclusion I have described to you, you must come and enjoy it speedily: and for this reason. On one side of me is a beautiful marble villa, with immense gardens and long winding walks ; and on the other side, with immense gardens also, is a large disused hotel, whose proprietors last year were bankrupt. It is built like an old château. It has quaint vanes on the gables ; and flights of marble steps lead up to the doors and windows. It is just at the cape's point ; and its domain of gardens, with their long walks and terraces, and their arches of trellised roses, are bounded on three sides by the sea. Those gardens, silent and lifeless, not a soul but the gardeners now walks in them—the gardeners and myself, and, who should you think besides ? Poor Frederic Stanley—the cleverest of our Oxford idlers ; who, since we knew him, has been first a guardsman, and is now a Catholic priest.

How time does change some men! Stanley
is here for his health : he is broken down
with work. He looks, I fancy, rather ask-
ance at me ; but we have often little reserved
conversations together.

' However I am wandering from the point.
What I want to tell you is this. Up till now
the hotel and the villa have been alike
tenantless, and I have been able to use both
gardens as my own ; but that happy period
is now drawing fast to a close. Some
English people, whose names I do not know,
though no doubt I shall soon make their
acquaintance, are coming, or perhaps have
already come, to the villa. And as to the
hotel, what do you think has happened ?
Our friend the Duchess has taken it—it is
still furnished—for the whole of next month,
and intends having a large party there. So
you see that very soon I shall be saying
good-bye to solitude. This last piece of news

I have only this instant learned, and from the Duchess herself. I can't exactly say if I am glad or sorry. I shall have at all events a very enlivening neighbour; and her company always charms me. It is not the charm now, as it must once have been, of beauty and sentiment. It is what at fifty supplies their place, and rivals them; it is the charm of mundane humour. This bright, gay humour of feminine middle-age, it always seems to me, is a very rare gift. It is a highly artificial product, and is almost peculiar, I think, to one class of society. It requires to develop it a combination of two things in the past—the susceptibilities of the world of romance, and the indulgence of them in the word of fashion. However, be our friend's charm what it will, I am at this moment going to enjoy it; as in another five minutes I shall be at dinner with her.

And this at last brings me to a con

fession which will amuse you. Where do
you think I am writing you this letter? Not
in my philosophic garden, not in my quiet
study. All about me is gas-light and gilding,
and a murmur of garish life. The figures
surrounding me are gamblers and Parisian
cocottes; and I am breathing, not the scent of
the sea or of flowers, but of patchouli and
faint stale cigarette smoke. I am in the
reading-room at Monte Carlo. I drove over
here this morning—or rather, my coachman
drove me—partly to try a new pair of horses,
and partly for the sake of the starlight drive
back again. The Duchess is staying for a
day or two at the hotel attached to the
gambling-rooms, and it seems she has a little
dinner party every night in the restaurant.
To-night the Grantlys are coming. You
remember Grantly at Oxford? He is now
in the First Life Guards; and his wife is a
lovely American, whose face is even prettier

than her dresses, and, if possible, even more changing.

'*À propos* of the women here, there is one on the sofa opposite me, who is really divinely lovely. Whenever I look up from my writing, I am met by her soft large eyes, half sad and half voluptuous in their tenderness. She is as different from the women near her as day from night, or rather as the stars from gas-light. She is one of the fallen; I fear there can be no doubt about that; but refinement—even a sort of nobleness—can outlive virtue. There is not a touch of paint on her; and her dress, which fits her perfectly, is strangely simple. If I have any skill in reading the looks of women, there is something of a higher life yet lingering in that soft, pleading face, that she half hides from me by her large crimson fan. Some women have a glance that makes me long to talk to them, just as clear sea-water makes me long to plunge in it.

'Write to me soon. I am obliged to stop now.

'By the way, besides the Grantlys, there is another guest expected, who is to me more interesting. I mean Lord Surbiton. He was the first man of letters I ever knew; and when I was seventeen, he seemed to me little short of a god.

'Good-bye; I must be going. My fair one is rising too.'

CHAPTER III.

THE Duchess's stately figure was familiar at Monte Carlo, and many an eye followed her as she entered the gorgeous restaurant.

'Garçon,' she said, as she took her seat at the large table reserved for her, '*Pommery et gréno, extra sec*—the last champagne on the wine list. You must put three bottles in ice instantly, for in five minutes we shall be quite ready for dinner. And—wait, wait a moment, man, for I have not done speaking to you— we are not going to pay thirty-six francs again for a single dish of asparagus ; so you

D

will perhaps have the goodness to recollect
that. And you must lay another place if you
please, as we shall be five dining this evening
instead of four.'

Captain and Mrs. Grantly appeared
almost immediately, and with them was an
elderly man in close attendance on the latter.
The young guardsman and his wife were a
very characteristic couple, and looked like a
bright embodiment of the spirit of modern
London. The appearance of their companion was very different. His dress was
too showy for what is now correct taste, and
his jewelled scarf-pin and sleeve-links were
both of enormous size. But on him these
splendours seemed to lose half their offensive-
ness. They were plainly the *fashion* of a
past generation, not the *vulgarities* of the
present one : they even heightened by contrast the strange effect of his face, with its
worn weary cheeks, and his keen glance like

an eagle's. This was none other than the renowned Lord Surbiton—the poet, diplomat, and dandy who had charmed the last generation.

The whole party had been winning largely at the tables, and their spirits were quite in keeping with the glittering scene around them. The crowd which filled the restaurant was to-night even more gay than usual. All the men were at least dressed like gentlemen, and most of the women were far more splendid than ladies. Fashionable exiles from the English world of fashion were detected in numbers by the amused eyes of the Duchess ; and with them the fair companions who had caused their exile or were sharing it. It was said even that royalty was not absent, and that there thus was a divine element unrecognised in the midst of the human. Everywhere there was a flashing of restless eyes and diamonds ; furred and embroidered

opera-cloaks were being disposed of over the
backs of chairs ; long gloves were being
unbuttoned and drawn off; and white hands,
galncing with rings, were composing deranged
tresses.   Above was the arched ceiling glowing with gold and pictures; and the walls,
florid with ornament, returned every shaft of
lamplight from the depths of immense mirrors,
or the limbs of naked goddesses.

' Now, this,' said the Duchess, ' is exactly
what I enjoy : charming company, a charming scene before one, and—let me tell you
ail, for I myself ordered it—a really excellent
dinner.   However,' she went on, as she
unfolded her napkin, and looked with a slow
smile at the *menu*, ' we must be temperate in
the midst of plenty ; for remember, Mrs.
Grantly, you and I and your husband are to
go back to the tables again for one half-hour
afterwards—only one half-hour, mind ; and
then, as Lord Surbiton suggests—he is always,

as we all know, poetical—we will have our coffee outside, and compose our feelings under the stars of heaven.'

' What!' said Mrs. Grantly, 'and is Lord Surbiton not coming back to the rooms with us ? '

' Not he,' said the Duchess. ' He's not half a man at gambling. I don't think your poets ever are. But where,' she exclaimed presently, as she saw that a chair was vacant, ' where is Mr. Vernon ? Has any one seen our Mr. Ralph Vernon ? We can't possibly get on without our one unmarried young . man ; though, to say the truth, till this moment I had quite forgotten to miss him.'

' Mr. Vernon !' echoed Mrs. Grantly with a laugh. ' I'd advise you, Duchess, not to count upon him. I saw him on the hotel steps only ten minutes ago, and what do you think he was doing ? Why, he was talking to that beautiful creature we were all admiring

at the tables—the woman with the red fan
and the long dark eyelashes. I don't know
what she was saying, I'm sure, but she had
her hand on his arm, and he was bending
down to her.'

'Oh, ho——' began the Duchess, with a
soft low laugh. But Lord Surbiton interrupted her.

'Vernon!' he said; 'can this be the
Ralph Vernon that I once knew, some thir-
teen years ago—a dreamy eager boy, who
used to come and show me his poetry?'

'To be sure it is,' said the Duchess.
'Poetry, painting, and heaven knows what
else—I believe he has tried all of it.'

'Ah!' said Lord Surbiton; 'I once had
great hopes of him. I once thought he was
signed with the veritable sign of genius.'

'Well,' replied the Duchess, 'and he *is*
very clever, I believe.'

'Men who are clever,' said Lord Surbiton

solemnly, 'we can count by millions: men with genius we count by units. As for Vernon, his early verses were beautiful, in spite of their crude language. They had the same charm in them that his ideal eyes had—little of the gladness of youth, but all its sweetness and its hunger.'

'It seems,' said the Duchess, 'that this is a young man who is very much to be envied; for in addition to all these charms, he has two others that women think irresistible—a fortune and a history.'

'Yes,' said Lord Surbiton, with a wave of his jewelled hand; 'women are always attracted by a man with a history, because it always means that he is to be either blamed or pitied.'

'And what,' said Mrs. Grantly, 'may Mr. Vernon's history be?'

'Ah!' said the Duchess, 'that's just what we don't know, and that's the very reason

why we find it so interesting. Never be too
curious, my dear, about a friend's history;
and then you can always stick up for him
with a clear conscience.'

'Look!' exclaimed Mrs. Grantly, 'here
the charmer comes. I only hope he won't
be trying all his fascinations on me.'

Vernon was full of regrets for being behind his time; but these he discovered were
met with nothing but laughter. Mrs. Grantly
assured him at once that they knew all about
him and his doings. 'And this is the man,'
she went on—' now, I ask you all to look at
him—who says he has come abroad for the
sake of philosophic solitude!'

'And why not?' said Vernon; 'I think
I am quite consistent. Solitude is my wife,
and society is my mistress; and I like to live
with the one, and be always intriguing with
the other.'

'Well,' exclaimed Mrs. Grantly, 'since

we are your society for the moment, our collective place in your heart is, I must say, not very honourable.'

'Never mind about that,' said the Duchess. 'What my suspicions rest upon is Mr. Vernon's solitude—that retiring villa of his at the Cap de Juan : especially now we hear all this about red fans, and whisperings, and hotel door-steps, and long eyelashes.'

'My attentions on the door-step,' said Vernon, 'were of the strictly Platonic order. There is something rather touching in that woman, when one comes to talk to her.'

'Very likely,' said Captain Grantly drily ; 'there always is. *Touching* is the exact word for it. And what's her rank, Vernon ? Is she a princess or a duchess ? '

'If she's a princess,' said Vernon, 'she must have lost her principality ; for she was dreadfully in want of a thousand francs to gamble with.'

'Very likely,' said Captain Grantly ; 'they
all are.'

The Duchess, meanwhile, was surveying
the motley scene before her. ' I confess,' she
said with a soft smile of amusement, 'this is
hardly the place one would come to if one
were in search of Platonic attachments.
Now, look round, all of you, and take stock
of the company. There are plenty of men
one knows—of course, one expects that ; but
the women with them—did you ever see anything like it ? Come, Mr. Vernon, you
understand these things. Just observe the
couple behind you—they can't talk English,
so we needn't mind discussing them—are
they man and wife, do you think ? Or that
fine lady, with the hair sprinkled with gold-
dust, whom Lord Surbiton seems to admire
so—what relation should you say she was to
the old Jew she is dining with ? Upon my
word, Mrs. Grantly,' she added presently, ' I

don't believe that, our two selves excepted, there's a single woman here you could possibly call respectable.'

'That's the very reason,' said Mrs. Grantly, 'why I like being here so much. It makes me feel like an angel. But talking of angels, there goes a genuine one, if you like, for you; there goes Colonel Stapleton. Oh my! and isn't he grown fat and ugly! You'd never have thought—would you?— that that man was once the best dancer in London. And, Duchess,' she went on, 'I hope you admire the big checks on his coat. 'Twould take four of him, I guess, to play one game of chess upon.'

Colonel Stapleton was a florid man of it might be five-and-forty. Despite his inclination to stoutness, he held himself well and gracefully, and had an air about him of dissolute good-breeding. He had one other charm, too, of which Vernon was at once

made sensible—a taking and very musical
voice, which, as he stopped for a moment to
speak to a friend dining, could be heard
distinctly at the Duchess's table. ' The one
with the red fan ? ' he was saying gaily ;
' yes, she, if you like it, is a regular out-and-
outer. She's down here, so she tells me, with
some fellow who belongs to the " Figaro." '

Vernon and Captain Grantly both over-
heard this. The former was somewhat
annoyed, and the latter amused at it, though
he was at the same time frowning over his
wife's late observations. ' Poor old Jack
Stapleton ! ' he said ; ' Jessie can't bear him,
though I'm sure I don't know why. He's as
good-hearted a fellow as ever lived, and is
nobody's enemy but his own.'

' To be sure,' said the Duchess. ' We all
of us know Jack Stapleton. If he was a
little bit thinner, your wife would be only too
delighted with him.'

Mrs. Grantly, however, was by no means silenced.

'Look at his back,' she said, 'as he's sitting down to his dinner. Isn't selfishness written in every curve of it? The way'—she went on, as she leant over to the Duchess—'the way that man behaved to a young girl I know is something more than words can describe to you.'

'Jessie!' exclaimed her husband sharply, as if determined to change the subject, 'look behind you for a minute. There's the old hag—don't you see her?—who tried to collar your money this afternoon at the tables. It's worth while watching her just to see how she claws her wine-glass.'

'I hadn't observed her,' said the Duchess. 'Well, she at any rate has no compromising diamonds, and no wicked Lothario to attend to her.'

Mrs. Grantly's eye lit up with a sudden

laughter. 'Lord Surbiton,' she said, as she
touched his arm with her fan, and pointed
out the old woman in question, 'I guess I
can show you one virtuous woman here.
Her morals, I am sure, are strictly unim-
peachable. I'll lay you six to one on them
in black-silk stockings.'

Lord Surbiton eyed Mrs. Grantly with
a look of somewhat sinister gallantry. 'If
your feet and ankles,' he said, 'are as lovely
as your hands and wrists, I shall proudly pay
the bet, even if I have the sad fortune to
win it.'

'In that case,' said Mrs. Grantly drily,
'I shall ask you to make your bets with my
husband. If you will do so with him on the
same principle next Ascot, we shall still
manage, perhaps, to keep out of the work-
house.'

Mrs. Grantly, though she said what she
chose herself, could always hold her own to

perfection; and Lord Surbiton's gaze was now at once withdrawn from her. But a few minutes afterwards, when he again turned to her, there was a change in his whole expression that she was not prepared for. His worn face, as a friend had once observed of him, was like a battered stage on which the scenery was always shifting; and it now had a strange appearance, as of some ruinous transformation-effect. Every trace of its late look had gone from it: it gleamed, instead, with a grave uncertain tenderness, like a light from a lost boyhood; and even his artificial manner when he spoke did not destroy the impression.

'You have shown me,' he said, 'one virtuous woman. Let me now show you another. Do you see the two who have this moment entered?'

The eyes of all the party were turned in

the same direction. There was no mistaking
for an instant who it was that had attracted
him. Standing close to the door, and looking
about her in some uncertainty, was a tall
English girl, in company of an elder lady.
The two had apparently come there to dine,
and, being strange to the place, did not know
where to bestow themselves. The girl's
hesitation, however, could scarcely be called
embarrassment. The scene seemed to distress far more than to embarrass her; though
it would hardly have been unnatural if it had
done both. There was a proud reserve, however, in her graceful movements and attitude,
which, amongst such surroundings, sufficed
at once to distinguish her. She was very
pale, with a brow and throat like a magnolia
blossom ; only her lips, in the words of
Solomon, seemed by contrast 'a thread of
scarlet ;' and her large clear eyes were dark
as the darkest violet. She stood there in

the glare and glitter like a creature from another world.

Lord Surbiton broke silence in slow, measured accents. 'It looks,' he said, 'as if an angel had descended in the midst of us, like a snow-flake.'

There was a pause. The apparition astonished the whole party. Vernon's eyes, in especial, were fixed intently on her.

'Angel or no angel,' said the Duchess presently, 'I can see, even from this distance, that she gets her clothes, not from heaven, but Paris: and nothing costs so much as well-made angelic simplicity. However joking apart,' she added, and more seriously 'upon my word I quite agree with Lord Surbiton. It is literally an angel's face; and a very high-bred angel's into the bargain. But, good gracious!—what a place to bring her to!'

Suddenly the two strangers were observed

to move forward into the room, while the younger one first started, and then broke into a smile.

' Look!' said the Duchess with interest, ' they have evidently found some one they know here. Let us try and discover who it is.'

' Oh my!' exclaimed Mrs. Grantly, ' I can see who: and—would you believe it?—why, it's Colonel Stapleton! Duchess, you don't know what you missed. You should have seen how he jumped up when he saw them, like a beer-barrel on springs! And there's your angel, Lord Surbiton—there she is, shaking hands with him. Well, all I can say is, that I wish her joy of her company.'

' Come, Mr. Vernon,' said the Duchess, as dinner drew to a close, ' you seem very silent and abstracted. This interesting young lady has clearly made an impression on you.'

' Haven't you noticed him?' said Mrs.

Grantly; 'he's been watching her all the time; and I can tell by his face that he's jealous of Colonel Stapleton. However, Mr. Vernon, there is one crumb of comfort for you; she has not been dining at the same table with him.'

'No,' said Captain Grantly, 'but she's looked round and smiled at him every ten minutes. Keep yourself calm, Vernon, and don't go calling old Jack out for it.'

'I should think,' said Vernon, with a gravity he was quite unconscious of, 'that they are relations of some kind or other—cousins,' he went on meditating, 'cousins probably, or perhaps even niece and uncle.'

'Capital!' exclaimed the Duchess. 'He's thought the whole matter out to himself. Mr. Vernon, your tastes are, I must say, most versatile. You begin the dinner with Venus, and you wind it up with Diana. But tell me,' she went on, as she pushed her chair back, and sedately prepared to rise, 'are you a gambler as well as a lover ?   For if not, you will perhaps smoke here with Lord Surbiton, while we three go back to the tables for a little ; and then we will all meet presently outside for our coffee.'

CHAPTER IV.

LEFT *tête-à-tête* with Vernon, Lord
Surbiton fixed his eyes on him,
drawing meanwhile from his
pocket a gorgeous gold cigarette case.
'That tobacco,' he said solemnly through the
soft smoke-puffs, 'which has the subtlest of all
aromas, was grown amongst the haunted hills
of Syria.' This probably may have been true
enough : he omitted to add, however, that he
had bought it himself in a spot no more
haunted than Bond Street. But the old elaborate manner which had once impressed
Vernon, now again arrested him ; though his

eyes had still been straying in the direction of
the fair stranger.

'It is a long time,' went on Lord Surbiton, 'since I last saw you; or to one, young
as you are, it must seem long.'

'I like to be called young,' said Vernon,
'for I have at least one sign of age in me,
and that is I am beginning to value my
youth.'

'Happy philosopher,' cried the other,
'who can value the treasure while you still
possess it! When last I saw you, you were
just leaving Eton, and you had not learnt
such wisdom then. You came to me one
morning before luncheon, sad and eager, with
some verses of yours, that you might ask
what a poet thought of them. I suggested
that you should read them aloud to me, but
you were too modest to do so; so I took
them myself, and read them aloud to you.
When I had finished I looked up, and there

were two large tears trembling in my young bard's eyes.'

'What!' exclaimed Vernon, 'and do you really remember that unfortunate boyish stuff of mine?'

'Boy,' said Lord Surbiton, 'your verses were *not* stuff; and there are certain things which *I* never forget—

> Oh Goddess, I am sick at heart, o'erworn
> With weariness,
> For the weight of life is bitter to be borne
> Companionless.

That is how your verses began: you see I can quote them still. Professedly, they were a sort of prayer to Diana: but really they were far more than that. They were the voice of youth that is heard through all the ages—youth crying in its solitude for some high companionship. There is nothing, Vernon, so unutterably melancholy as a boy's passionate purity: and for me you were then the symbol of the eternal longing of boyhood.'

'How well,' said Vernon,' I remember
that little poem of mine, though I confess I
am surprised that you do! I remember the
day I wrote it, and the sound of it still rings
in my ears; but there is one thing wanting—
one thing quite gone from me—and that is the
sort of longing I meant to express in it. My
thoughts and my aspirations of those days
have become a mystery to myself. I am
startled to find sometimes how utterly I have
lost the clue to them.'

'That is always the way,' said Lord
Surbiton, 'when life is still developing,
and one form of eagerness succeeds and
dispossesses another. It is in virtue
of this process that you now see your
youth to be valuable. In the middle age
of your boyhood you longed sadly for
the unattainable; in the boyhood of your
middle age, you idealise the attainable.
Happy philosopher, I again say to you—philo-

sopher, lover, poet, and man of the world in one !'

' I doubt,' said Vernon smiling, ' if I now idealise anything ; and I fear, Lord Surbiton, that you idealise me. I am no longer a lover, nor even a would-be poet.'

' Not a poet on paper, it may be ; but a poet in the way life touches you, and in the demands you make on it. To be a poet in this sense, you need never have written a line ; and yet the name may fit you, without any violence to its meaning. The imagination is for every man the co-creator of his universe, and those men are poets whose imaginations create most gloriously. And yet, my dear Vernon, you say you no longer idealise ! I shall as soon believe that as that you are no longer a lover. Why, within this last couple of hours, you have been making love to one lady, and longing, we all thought, to make love to another.'

'Ah !' said Vernon ; 'but the excitement
of making love is very different from the still
devotion of loving. What I have ceased to
be capable of, what I have lost even the power
of imagining, is a single passion that shall
sway or fulfil one's life. Love seems to me
now to be very much like temper. Your
dearest friend can irritate you into the one ;
the most commonplace woman can trick you
into the other : and you adore in the latter
case, and you accuse and abuse in the former,
in a way which by-and-by you can only
stupidly wonder at. I do not want to speak
cynically about this. A cynic is a foolish
fellow who either is ignorant, or pretends to
be, of a good third of an average man's
motives—those that are not contemptible ;
and I know that love, as a fact, can be pure
and true and faithful, and that it is really to
many the one thing worth living for. I only
speak for myself ; and all that I can see in

it is a passionate perversity both of judgment and of feeling. It exaggerates the
value of the special individual, just as
cynicism does the opposite for the race in
general. The concentrated praise is as false
as the diffused censure. Each is equally
silly to the eye of the calm judgment. My
wish now is for no emotion but such as
I can master. I wish to possess myself,
not to appropriate others ; and with regard to
women I agree with the poet Donne—

> I can love her and her, and you and you ;
> I can love any, so she be not true.'

' I did not expect,' said Lord Surbiton,
' when I called you a lover, to find you still
content at thirty with the intangible charms
of a moon-goddess. As we live on, we are
obliged to take the attainable, and do our
best to idealise that. You say you are not
constant. Well, no true artist is ; and you
have the artist's temper, I see, just as you

have the poet's—two things which by no
means always go together : indeed to unite
them is a rare triumph of character. Many
poets perhaps might have drawn a Des-
demona : only an artistic poet could have
drawn an Iago also. What marks the poetic
temper is the intensity of its sympathy;
what marks the artistic is the versatility.
The artist not only feels much, but he also
feels many things ; and in this way he
always preserves his balance. Every one
at the beginning has had the makings of
several characters in him. The artist has
the makings of an indefinite number. Most
men, farther out of their possible characters,
harden or settle down into one, but the artist
never does ; for character is nothing but
prejudice or trick grown permanent, and the
artist has no character, just as the chameleon
is said to have no colour. Thus when vulgar
critics declare with regard to some artistic

writer's creations—as often and often they
have done with regard to mine, for instance—
" Here are his own feelings ; he has drawn this
man from himself," they are at once right
and wrong. He has not only drawn *this* man
from himself, but he has drawn all ; for he
becomes himself some new man to be drawn
from, every time he suppresses some newly-
combined nine-tenths of himself. This, Vernon, is the true artistic versatility ; and her
Grace—who by the way is an uncommonly
shrewd woman—at once saw you possessed
it. You can respond in the same half-hour,
she told you, to the beauty of Diana and of
Venus. Such versatility is the true elixir of
youth ; it makes even the wisdom of age
supple. My dear fellow,' he said, somewhat coming down from his pedestal, ' constancy, though we know its value for most
men, is the elixir of middle age. It makes you
five-and-forty at once, and it keeps you there.'

Vernon at this moment let his eye wander, and a sudden exclamation broke from him which at once put a stop to philosophy.

'Damn it!' he said, 'we have been talking of dead Dianas; and meanwhile the living one has taken flight, and deserted us.'

Lord Surbiton turned his head, and saw that the fair stranger and her companion had gone. Where feminine beauty was concerned, he was always prompt and practical; and he at once set about rising, though his movements were somewhat slow.

'She can't have gone far,' he said. 'We shall be sure to see her again somewhere; and her Grace, or Captain Grantly, will find out all about her for us. Or failing these, there is that fellow, Stapleton.'

He took Vernon's arm with a sedate and leisurely dignity, and the two left the restaurant. They paused in the cloak-room

which is just outside, and Lord Surbiton was
being helped by a garçon into a magnificent
sable overcoat, when a female figure appeared, with a look that at once attracted him.
This was none other than the lady of the red
fan. She had come for her opera-cloak;
and before Vernon was even aware of her
presence, Lord Surbiton, with as quick a
gallantry as his years permitted him, was
arranging it tenderly for her, over her finely-
shaped shoulders.

He was sufficiently delighted with his
performance thus far; but a still greater
pleasure awaited him. The lady cast a
glance at him with her soft, appealing eyes,
and murmured, '*Merci, milord.*' She did
not blush, but she looked much as if she
wished to do so. Lord Surbiton at once
laid his hand on his heart, and was begging
to be told how he was honoured by madame
knowing him. 'Ah!' she replied, 'and need

a renowned man ask ? Why, the poems and
the romances of monsieur are as much read
in Paris as in London.' Here she caught
sight of Vernon; and, with the quietest
smile in the world, ' I am going,' she went
on, ' once more to the tables. Will not you
two come, and join your luck with mine ? '

Lord Surbiton was completely charmed
with her, and regretted not a little that to do
this was impossible. He was almost aware
of a slight pang of jealousy when she bid
Vernon to put in more securely a diamond
pin that had become loose in her hair.

Vernon's hands lingered over the soft
brown plaits. ' You are very lovely,' he
said, ' though, of course, you don't need to
be told that ; and my morals will let you
play with my heart, though my prudence, I
fear, will not let you play with my fortune.'

He was in the middle of uttering this,
when he glanced aside for a moment, and his

eyes met those of the girl to seek whom he
had just risen from the dinner-table.   It was
but a glance she gave him ; and then her fair
head was averted : but the glance and the
gesture were only too expressive to him.
She seemed at once to comprehend and be
surprised at the scene he was taking part in,
and to turn away from it with contempt, pain,
and aversion. A disagreeable sense of shame
at once came over him ; nor were his reflections made pleasanter by what he observed
next moment.   As the girl, with her companion, was quitting the cloak-room, he was
just able to see her face light up for an
instant ; and directly afterwards Colonel
Stapleton entered.

The Colonel seemed almost as versatile
as Lord Surbiton himself ; for he was quite
as familiar with the fair Aspasia as he had
been a moment before with the pale and
virginal stranger. Vernon and Lord Surbiton

had been conversing with the former lady in French; and his lordship, who was somewhat deaf, had pronounced her accent perfect. The Colonel, however, to whom she turned instantly, composedly addressed some chaff to her in the homeliest English possible; and she with an equal fluency, though with a strong foreign twang, replied, 'If you don't look out, I shall smack your nasty little head for you.'

Vernon started at this astounding utterance, as if an adder had stung him. 'Good Heavens!' he exclaimed to himself, 'what an absolute fool I am!' And not without some *brusquerie*, which the fair one mistook for jealousy, he succeeded in withdrawing Lord Surbiton, and making a hasty exit. 'Her French,' he muttered, 'may be the French of the Faubourg, but her English is very certainly the English of Regent Street.'

Lord Surbiton, however, had completely

missed the above piece of *badinage* ; and pausing on the hotel door-steps, and laying his hand upon Vernon's arm, ' What a woman that is !' he exclaimed, with a slow gravity. ' It is in her class, after all, that the soul of the old world still lives on, with its passion, its grace, and its intellect ; and we, in our barbarous virtue, actually affect to look down on her. A woman like that ought to have lived at Athens, and have had a Pericles for her companion, and a Socrates for her pupil.'

Vernon made no response to this. His thoughts were still busy with those clear eyes that had humbled him. ' So much,' he said bitterly to himself, ' for a woman's power of insight ! She looks nothing but scorn at me, and yet smiles like a sister at that fat, sensual beast there !'

Before long Lord Surbiton began again, as they went in the direction where they expected to find their party. 'Ah, my dear Vernon !' he said, drawing a deep sigh that made his satin necktie creak, 'it is the artist's gift——' Here he paused for a moment to eye critically two young ladies who passed him. ' It is the artist's gift,' he resumed, 'to discern between good and evil ; it is his doom to be the servant of neither. He surveys life as a Cæsar surveyed the circus : and the affections and lusts of men can say nothing to him but *morituri te salutant.* He belongs to a middle race who are neither divine nor human, and he cannot really ally himself with any human being. This is why, when he dies, there are no flowers strewn on his tomb—no rosemary for remembrance, or pansies for tender thoughts ; but only the bloomless laurel—the leaf, not of love, but of homage.'

' Lord Surbiton '—it was the voice of the Duchess—'when you've done quoting poetry, you'll find us all here, ready for you to discover us.' She was seated with the Grantlys outside the café, at a round table laden with cups and liqueur-glasses. 'See,' she went on, 'we have ordered everything, and we have been so thoughtful that we have even kept chairs for you.'

'It seems to me,' said Lord Surbiton, 'that your Grace has kept two a-piece for us.'

'Ah!' said the Duchess, laughing, 'those two other chairs are for some particular friends of mine, whom I asked just now to come and have their coffee with us. Now, Mr. Vernon, here is a riddle for you. Who should you think these particular friends are? Why, your fair paragon of the restaurant, and the old lady, her aunt. I met them five minutes ago, as we were coming here from the gambling-rooms, and it flashed on me all of a sudden who the aunt was. You, Lord

Surbiton, will remember her. She's the widow of Sir Edward Walters, who was our Minister for so many years at Stuttgart; and the girl—I remember her too quite well now— is that beautiful Cynthia Walters, who was made such a fuss about in London three seasons ago, and then got ill, and has never appeared since. Her home, it seems, is now with her aunt in Florence.'

'Look out, Duchess,' said Captain Grantly. 'Here they are coming.'

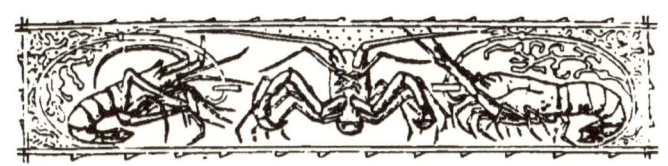

CHAPTER V.

LADY WALTERS was a woman of great sweetness of manner, yet with a touch now and then of subdued humour. She produced the impression that she had once known the world, but that she hardly knew it now ; for knowledge of the world can be forgotten like other knowledge, and from certain gentle natures it slips away easily.

She and Lord Surbiton had an extremely friendly greeting, and settled down at once into a talk over old days. As for Vernon

his position was less comfortable. The
Duchess introduced him to Miss Walters,
who had at first been unaware of his presence:
but the instant she recognised him the smile
died on her lips, and she acknowledged his
bow as coldly as any young lady of fashion
who seems to deny an acquaintance in the
very act of formally making it.

Vernon felt utterly worsted by her perfect
savoir faire; and what added not a little to
his suffering was that the Duchess should
witness his discomfiture, without knowing
what he felt sure was the cause of it. Too
proud or self-conscious to risk any further
repulse, he listened silently to the girl's
answers, as the Duchess put her through a
rapid catechism. 'We have taken,' she said,
'a villa beyond Nice, in the country. We
arrived but three days ago, from Florence.
We came over here this afternoon for the
music; but missed our train back again, and

so had to remain for dinner. I don't know
what we should have done if Colonel Stapleton, whom I have known from a child, had
not secured a table for us. I think this place
horrible. I was here once before, and I
detested it.'

Vernon watched her intently as she was
giving these answers. The moments were
few; but to him they were like a long dream.
He seemed to become familiar with all the
folds of her drapery, and each outline of arm
or figure that her dress revealed or hinted at.
There was a subtle air with her of fastidious
fashion, from her hat to her pointed shoes
and the long black gloves concealing her
dainty hands. But this was not all, or at
any rate Vernon thought not. She seemed
not only a woman of fashion, but a woman
of fashion who had the soul of a sibyl in her;
and her clear eyes seemed touched with some
high wistful melancholy.

The impression she made on the Duchess was different. Her Grace had found Miss Walters somewhat chilly in manner ; so she brought her questions pretty soon to a close, and addressed herself to Mrs. Grantly. Vernon hoped with trembling that now might be his chance : but no, it was not to be. Miss Walters turned away from him, and seemed lost in the scene before her. That scene was one which is certainly unique in Europe, and it was now wearing its strangest and most striking aspect. The large *place*, with its gleaming buildings round it, was a lake of transparent shadow, dotted with countless gas-lamps, and full of the vague whispers of fountains and human life. On one side flared the hotel they had lately quitted ; on another the great casino, pale like a skeleton from globes of electric light. On another, where the buildings were lower and more broken, tall palms might be seen, with their plumes in the clear sky; and beyond were balustrades of marble, and spaces of dark sea: whilst behind and in grim contrast rose the barren towering mountains, and dwarfed the world at the foot of them into a small cluster of fire-flies.

Lord Surbiton had been on the watch to attract Miss Walters's attention, and he now saw his opportunity.

' This place,' he said as he fixed his eyes on her, ' always seems to me like the moral sewer of Europe—a great drain's mouth open at the foot of the hills. There is a tragic irony even in its loveliness.'

' Tragic or not,' said the Duchess, ' we have had a most amusing dinner here; haven't we, Mrs. Grantly? Though I'm sure I've forgotten by this time what it was we were talking about.'

' A proof,' said Lord Surbiton, ' of how well your Grace was conversing. True conversation is like good champagne. It exhilarates for the moment, but next morning we feel no trace of it.'

Vernon here broke silence. ' If true conversation,' he said, 'is like good champagne, true love is like bad. False and true love may seem just the same when we taste them. We only detect the true when we find that our head aches afterwards.'

' That,' said Lord Surbiton, still looking towards Miss Walters, ' is why a serious passion is so great an educator. But its work only begins when the pain it causes has left us. Strong present feeling narrows our sympathies ; strong past feeling enlarges them. Thus a woman of the world always should have been, but should never be, in love. She should always have had a grief : she should never have a grievance.'

'Why,' asked Miss Walters coldly, ' do you say this of a woman of the world especially ? '

'Because it is only in the world, or in what we call society, that intercourse with our fellows is really a completed fine art. It there *is* what elsewhere it only pretends to be. Men who profess to think gravely or to have grave ends speak of society as the type of what is vain and frivolous. Perhaps they are right—who knows? Yet society is the logical end of the whole of this world's civilisation; and of all the follies that I ever set any store by, fashion is the one I could still find most to say for. Fashion,' he continued, 'is the daintiest form of fame, and sometimes of power also; and were it only as wide and lasting as it is delicate, it would unite in itself the objects of all human ambitions.'

'Are the objects of ambition,' said Miss Walters, 'the chief objects of life?'

'Men in general,' said Lord Surbiton, 'are the puppets of three forces—ambition, love, and hunger; but love destroys the appetite; ambition destroys love; and fashion absorbs, or at any rate sways, ambition.'

These general maxims did not much delight the Duchess, and she betrayed at this juncture that her thoughts had been somewhat wandering.

'Captain Grantly !' she exclaimed, 'I wonder whose are those horses that are waiting there at the door of the casino— the pair of greys, I mean, in that rather smart-looking carriage. I watched them drive round, five minutes ago ; and the near one, do you know, is really a first-rate stepper.'

This profane nterruption put a stop to Lord Surbiton s eloquence, for Miss Walters turned round, and began to look at the horses : whilst her aunt, hearing a railway whistle, consulted her watch, and said they must soon be moving. 'However,' she added, 'there must be plenty of time yet, as

Colonel Stapleton said he would come and
see us safe to the station.'

'I, too,' said Vernon, 'am reminded to
think of moving; for I see my carriage is
already there waiting for me.'

'What!' said the Duchess, 'and is that
fine turn-out yours, Mr. Vernon? Well,
here's luxury for a young man of thirty!'

'By Gad, my dear chap, you *are* a swell,'
said Captain Grantly, putting his hand on
Vernon's shoulder.

Wealth has a certain power over those
even who are least touched by it. It calls
their attention to the man possessing it, if
only to make it worth their while to despise
him; and Vernon knew in an instant that
Miss Walters turned to glance at him. Once
again he was about to attempt speaking to
her, when he was interrupted by the arrival
of Colonel Stapleton.

'Here's a go!' cried the Colonel, panting

and out of breath, ' I've been looking for you, Lady Walters, for the last twenty minutes ; and now your train's gone, and you must stop the night here. If you'll let me, I'll get you rooms directly at the Hôtel de Paris. The Princesse de —— and the Prince for the time being have just cleared out unexpectedly ; so I know they can take you in, and we'll show Miss Cynthia a little more of the life here.'

' If you stop, you know,' said the Duchess, ' there is my maid who can look after you. I can lend you almost everything ; and you can buy a tooth-brush here.'

Miss Walters turned to Colonel Stapleton with a hasty frown. ' No—no,' she said ; ' let us do anything rather than that. This place is perfectly unendurable.'

Vernon observed her closely, and with extreme surprise. She spoke in a manner that would have been rudeness to any common acquaintance even of long standing, but the

Colonel, strange to say, was not in the least abashed by it ; he only eyed her with a look of quiet amusement. ' Come, little vixen,' he whispered, ' don't be naughty. I'm sure Aunt Louisa will give her vote for staying.'

But Lady Walters wished to do no such thing ; and she was already inquiring nervously if there would be any difficulty in getting a carriage. ' Come,' said Miss Walters, taking hold of Colonel Stapleton's sleeve, 'be good, and go and tell her about it. We mean to go somehow, so you may as well make yourself of use to us.'

He was forestalled, however, by Captain Grantly, who had at once volunteered to go off to the livery-stables, and was just starting when he was recalled by the practical Duchess. ' You may as well find out first,' she said, ' where it is Lady Walters wants to be driven to ; for at this time of night they will often refuse to take you.'

'Oh!' said Lady Walters, somewhat troubled by this, 'it is to the Cap de Juan. It is a long way by the road, I'm afraid. Perhaps, after all, we had better remain here.'

Vernon felt all the blood rush at once to his face; and for a moment his heart stopped beating.

'The Cap de Juan!' exclaimed the Duchess; 'why that settles, everything. Come Mr. Vernon, now is your opportunity. My dear Lady Walters, here is a young man with a carriage and horses ready, who is only too anxious to take you back to your very door-step.'

A rapid look of annoyance passed over Miss Walters' face. 'We couldn't think,' she said, with a cold politeness, 'of taking Mr. Vernon's horses so great a distance. He is hardly aware, perhaps, of the journey there is before us.'

'On the contrary,' said Vernon, 'I am

particularly well aware of it, for it is the very
journey that is also before me. If I am not
much mistaken, we are all but next-door
neighbours. Your house, I think, must be
the Château St. John ; and, if so, our two
gardens touch each other.'

After this there was nothing more to be
said. Circumstances had at length played
into Vernon's hands ; and another caprice in
his life was to be at least partially gratified.

'Well,' said the Duchess, as the carriage
drove off, ' I'm glad Mr. Vernon has got what
he wanted, though Miss Cynthia, at first, was,
I must say, very snubby to him. However,
one can never judge by this. Perhaps, when
we go to the Cap de Juan, we shall find them
an engaged couple. Who knows ? '

' I know,' said Mrs. Grantly, ' and I'll bet
you anything we shall not. A man like Mr.
Vernon will never marry. He's exactly,' she
added, dropping her voice, ' like a younger

edition of Lord Surbiton ; and I guess they're
a couple of shams—the two of them.'

' I think,' said the Duchess, ' that Mr.
Vernon is charming.'

' Yes—to know,' said Mrs. Grantly, ' but
not to depend upon.'

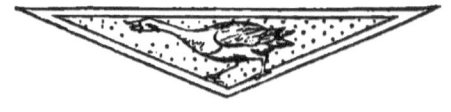

CHAPTER VI.

ERNON and his friends were meanwhile hastening homewards. Lady Walters had addressed to him a few kind civilities, eyeing him the while with a look of trustful friendliness ; but her niece had hardly said anything, and the three soon sank into silence. Every influence, indeed, seemed to persuade to it—the easy motion of the carriage, the rhythmic tramp of the horses, the soft fanning of the night air, and the pageant of sea and mountain that was sweeping past them like a dream. Here was a gaudy villa, surmounted by a huge coronet,

the home of some Russian gambler ; here,
with domes and minarets, a dwelling yet
more fantastic. Scents of flowers blew down
to them from the gardens ; and over the
garden walls hung spiked aloes and cactuses.
Then presently the scene grew wilder. On
the right, wooded gorges slanted up into the
mountains ; and on the left, the sea below
them broke into fairy bays. All this seemed
to absorb Miss Walters ; and her eyes being
thus occupied, Vernon was able unobserved
to observe her. He had once remarked in
one of his more delicate moods, that a woman
whose dress is the perfection of fashion, is
never herself the perfection of real refinement.
But he now felt inclined to modify this judgment. The vanities of this world seemed,
on the girl before him, as natural as its own
petals to some delicate hot-house flower ; so
that she was as little troubled by their possession as the saint is who has renounced them.

'The effect of her presence,' he wrote that night in his diary, 'was at once charming and singular. It did not at first concentrate my thoughts on herself; but it moved like a wind amongst them, and stirred them in all directions. Vague aspirations of many kinds awoke in me. I longed in grotesque rotation to make poetry, to ride hard, and to pray; and when something roused the aunt, and between two sleeps she talked a little to me, I was annoyed and jarred by having the silence broken.'

Lady Walters, it is true, had begun somewhat abruptly. 'What a pity it is,' she said, as though following up some train of thought of her own, 'that poor Jack Stapleton never married! He is naturally such a kind, good creature. It is self-indulgence that has ruined him.'

'And do you think,' said Vernon, 'that marriage will always save a man?'

'Not always,' she said, 'and it never affects a man as it does a woman. Yet some men, Mr. Vernon, are ruined for the want of it—often those with the warmest and sweetest natures. You know the man that his friends call a *good fellow*—who, like a sunflower always turns towards happiness. If such a man has a wife he cares for, he will live that he may make her happy ; but if left to himself, shall I tell you what will happen to him ? He will live, not to give pleasure but to find it ; and to like consorting with happy people is a very different thing from trying to make people happy.'

' Perhaps you are right,' said Vernon with a slight involuntary sigh. ' But how should you say that marriage affected women ?'

' Ah !' said Lady Walters, 'in another way entirely. When a woman marries with affection her whole character changes. She grows absorbed in the things that absorb her hus-

band ; and, through him, they become really
a new life to her.'

' If I thought of marrying,' said Vernon,
' it would be with a different hope. I should
hope to find a wife, who, if she had my
tastes at all, had had them before she knew
me ; and that her already possessing them
were a cause of her sympathy; not that her
acquiring them for my sake were the signs of
it. I should like her life to stand on its own
basis ; and in her pursuits I should like to
have a constant rival, that should keep my
affection fresh with a kind of stingless
jealousy.'

Lady Walters smiled at him incredulously,
with half-closed eyes. 'I am afraid, Mr.
Vernon,' she said, 'you've never been in love
yet.' Then the conversation dropped ; and
it was soon evident that she had again fallen
asleep. Vernon was pleased to have been
able to talk in Miss Walters' hearing, since

he found her so difficult of direct access ; and he now fancied that she looked a little less coldly at him. Presently she asked him of her own accord the name of some place they were passing. He answered her question ; but he found he could get no farther. In spite of himself he was still embarrassed in her presence. The remembrance that her first sight of him had been in the middle of his foolish scene with the Frenchwoman, abased him in his own estimation : he was in a thoroughly wrong position. He leaned his head back, and looked up at the stars, and was soon completely lost in another deep reverie. All of a sudden the tenor of his thoughts betrayed itself. He broke out aloud with a single line from *Hamlet* :—

Oh, what a rogue and peasant slave am I !

He spoke the words abstractedly, and for a second or two seemed not to know he had uttered them. Then he recollected himself,

and there might have been an awkward
moment, if Miss Walters with ready tact had
not come to the rescue.

' I know that line so well,' she said ; ' but
I can't remember where it comes from.'

' It is from *Hamlet*,' said Vernon, ' a play
I know by heart ; and I often catch myself
repeating bits aloud from it.'

With this there ensued a little conversation about Shakespeare, then about poetry
generally ; and matters very soon were pro-
ceeding more smoothly. Vernon had once
again found his footing. His thoughts, his
feelings, and his words began to flow freely
as usual ; and when he looked into Miss
Walters' eyes he found she did not avert
them. The character of the drive in a single
instant changed for him ; and it quickly became as delightful as it had been disappoint-
ing hitherto. To all intents and purposes he
was alone with this fair stranger ; and she

was visibly now beginning to take a certain interest in him. Gradually, too, he became aware that her presence had some magnetic effect upon him. Her hand, her lips, her eye, even the soft furs on her jacket, and the faint perfume from her handkerchief touched his being, and made the blood in his veins tingle : whilst at the same time all in him that was most refined or delicate, seemed suddenly to be coming uppermost under the attraction of her presence. The moral recoil from the low and frivolous to whatever was pure and delicate, was in itself a pleasing shock to the intellectual voluptuary : whilst the sense that he had to efface a bad impression gave double earnestness to his efforts to create a good one. To a man of Vernon's temperament an experience of this kind was a luxury.

And yet, on his part, there was no acting or insincerity. His goodness, to say the least of it, was as genuine as his evil; and his voice, his look, and his manner, as he now spoke to Miss Walters, were all instinct with a chivalrous and a quite natural reverence.

'I am so glad,' he said at last, 'that I happened to have my carriage, and was able to take you away from that horrid place there.'

'If you think the place horrid,' she said gently, 'why do you go yourself to it?'

'One might ask, I am afraid, that question about many things. I went there to-day for distraction—to escape from my own company. It did well enough to distract me: but one wishes to shake the dust off one's feet afterwards.'

'Like my question,' she said, 'that will apply to many things. But are you living quite alone out here?'

'Yes,' said Vernon, 'with no company but my books and thoughts; and, though I came here on purpose to be with these, I am glad sometimes to escape from them. I had hoped to have brought a friend with me; indeed, perhaps he may still come. The best escape from one's thoughts is a friend one is really fond of.'

'That is hardly a flattering light,' she said, 'in which to regard a friend. There are some unhappy people whose only chance of peace lies in forgetting themselves; but such people, I believe, have made themselves unfit for friendship. I look on a friend as a person who will help one to find, not to lose, oneself. If you want to lose yourself, you should always live in society, and agree with Lord Surbiton that life's highest reward is fashion.'

'Are you then,' said Vernon, 'not fond of society?'

'Of course for happy people society is a healthy thing; but how one mixes in it depends on one's own character. One can be the fashion, and yet not be oneself a fashionable, as one sees in the case of many of the greatest people in London. I may myself have been less in the world, perhaps, than most women of my age; but still I have seen plenty of smart society; indeed, I have several relations who seem to live for nothing else: and, so far as I can tell, nothing hardens the heart like fashion. To a genuine fine lady—who is a very different person, by the way, from a *grande dame*—it is a thing next to impossible to value character rightly.'

'And yet many of the qualities,' said Vernon, 'that secure most applause in society, are the fruits, as Lord Surbiton told us, of some deeper life in the past. Take singing, for instance: what an effect real expression has!—and to express feeling in song, the singer must himself have felt.'

'Perhaps so; and for that very reason

the most touching singing has sometimes almost disgusted me. What a use to make of some buried and sacred sorrow, to conjure its ghost up that it may secure a drawing-room triumph for us !'

'One may, of course,' said Vernon, ' exaggerate views like these, till they become false and fantastic. But I am quite sure you are right to some degree. To be always in society is to be always with mere acquaintances, and with acquaintances who like you for your least genuine qualities. I have met many a man, staying in country houses, who must have been sickened, as he went to bed, by what he had said or laughed at in the smoking-room ; and yet the night after he has done just the same. To be always in this way with the world, is to be always estranged from oneself ; and one's true self, like other sensitive creatures, will in time die of neglect, or at least be ruined by it.

'Do you remember,' said Miss Walters, 'what I said just now—that a true friend is a person with whom we can find, not lose ourselves? I,' she went on, with a sigh and a slight shudder, 'have had friends of two kinds —true and false; and they have both done all they could for me.'

She shuddered.

'Are you cold?' murmured Vernon, leaning forward and looking at her. 'Let me put that shawl over your shoulders for you.' No lover could have done the office with more tenderness, or at the same time with more respect. Then for a moment he laid his hand upon hers, and asked, 'Are you warmer now?' The look, the touch formed a new crisis in their relationship; and they both grew aware of this by a new tone in their voices. Vernon himself was surprised at what had passed. He had never thought she could have so softened towards him;

but he knew that it was so by her two words
as she thanked him. And now with a soft
sensation, he felt his heart expanding ; and
grave and secret thoughts welled up to his
lips, and began to demand utterance. Should
he go on and utter them, fixing his eyes on
hers ? To do so, he knew, would be an
exquisite self-indulgence. It would be like
a passionate mental kiss to the beautiful
creature opposite him. But for a moment
he vacillated ; and there was a short moral
struggle in him. Had he the right intention
that could make that kiss lawful ? Might
not the very feelings he wished to express
be wronged by his then expressing them ?
Was such mental passion as this, with its
spasm of self-abandonment, in reality much
better than its coarser physical counterpart ?
Conscience, however, was weak, and was
swept aside by impulse.

'Shall I tell you,' he said, 'why I have

come out here ?   I have lost my self, and I
wish to find it again.   I wish to see how I
stand with my conscience, and to know what
I really value.   This is a task in which no
friend can help one ; one must enter into one's
own chamber and be still, for it.   At present,
it seems to me sometimes that I hardly have
a self ; but I feel, like a man in a dream, that
I am being swept passively through changing
states of consciousness.   Some may be
pleasant enough, some dull and dreary ; but
they are all shadowy things ; I have no
abiding part in them, nor is one bound by any
chain to the other.   I seem to be swept
through them, just as we in this carriage are
being swept through this ghostly landscape.
What I want is. to wake myself from this idle
dream of the world, and to get back again to
the realities I was once familiar with.   Such
a waking is a long, weary process ; and a
friend's presence may soothe one in it though

he cannot help it forward. Is that,' he said,
looking at her, 'is that a wrong view of
friendship ? '

'It is not my view,' she said, 'but no one
can answer for another. If I had to seek a
self that was lost, I should like to have a
friend with me.'

'To encourage you, yes : but not to share
your labour. You, for instance, could not re-
arrange my life for me ; and yet it is a great
help to me, even this little talk I have had
with you. You and I are near neighbours
now. Do you think we shall ever become
friends ? '

She gave him for the moment no direct
answer, but murmured half abstractedly, ' I
wonder how far you have wandered.'

' That,' said Vernon, 'is what I want to
find out myself.'

After this there was a pause, whilst the
two sank back into their own reflections, and

the changing fields and trees, as the carriage hurried onwards, surrounded and swept away from them.

Miss Walters at length began again. 'Perhaps you are surprised,' she said with a faint smile, 'at hearing me talk so decidedly about the world, and society, and friendship.'

'You certainly talk,' said Vernon, 'as if you had had experience.'

'I *have* had experience,' she said. 'I have had much—too much—of it. I have been a gambler, amongst other things. I won more than two thousand pounds once at *trente et quarante*. Do you think that was very nice of me?' And she fixed her eyes on him with a look which he could not fathom. 'You see, if I hate Monte Carlo, it is not because gambling has ruined me. And now,' she went on, 'I am going to say one thing more, which sounds also like the maxim of a rather experienced person. It is an answer to what you asked me just now. I have little belief, as a rule, in friendships between men and women—I mean when both the people concerned have youth and imagination. One or the other gets generally more or less than was bargained for.'

'I shall be thankful,' said Vernon, 'for the very least you will give me. You would find me a very safe person. A man's days of friendship begin when his days of love are over; and I,' he went on, knowing that he was making love all the time, 'am in my days of friendship.'

'You and I then, perhaps, are exceptions to the general rule. There are exceptions. I can at least say this much for myself, that I am far more likely to be a friend than to have one.'

She said this with a curious unconscious bitterness that perplexed and startled Vernon.

'You must let me show you,' he murmured, 'that you are wrong there.'

She paused, and then said abruptly, ' I
hope you didn't mistake me. I didn't mean
that I thought you would fall in love with
me. Perhaps you are just as safe from that
sort of thing as I am.'

'You are very young,' said Vernon, ' to
be talking in that way.'

' Youth and age,' she said, 'should not be
counted by years. No nun dying a living
death in a nunnery could be more shut out
from all danger of love than I am—from all
hope and from all fear of it.'

After this there was silence, till Lady
Walters woke up, and Vernon soon afterwards was saying adieu to his friends on
their own door-step.

But the night was not yet done for him.
He had refused to enter ; he was anxious to
be by himself again ; and, having sent his

carriage away, he walked back through the gardens. In his own lamp-lit villa a delicate supper was prepared for him, but he did nothing more than taste it, and he went out again into the mellow night air. He was like a man who had eaten a sort of moral opium, and his breast was full of a sweet, fantastic tumult. There was a magical resurrection in him of the wild romance of boyhood. He leaned his elbow on a pale glistening balustrade, and looked out over the sea. 'Sea of Romance,' his unuttered thoughts began in him, 'once again you have your old charm for me. Inarticulate whispers of ambition, of passion, and of music float up to me from your enchanted surface. Sea of Southern moon and of Italian twilights, what eyes of famous lovers have looked out on you ! The most musical of the world's love-songs have mixed over you with the vesper breezes ! Pale, restless waves, rocking under

the stars of midnight, the limbs of the mermaids know you: the nautilus floats upon
your bosom! Yes, and in me, too, up from
the depths of my being, thoughts and longings
are rising that sing like mermaids. What do
they sing of? Is it of her eyes and lips?
Are they singing to her spirit that it may
stoop down to mine?' He turned back to
his garden. That, too, was enchanted. Were
Oberon and Titania holding revel there?
Bush and blossom seemed populous with
airy presences. Every passion, every pleasure of his life, became a separate fairy,
with its body some faint perfume, and its
dwelling-place some half-closed flower-bell.
In luxurious agitation he again returned to
his sea-view. Far away over the waters the
lights of Nice were glittering fair and distant
like a braid of golden stars. On a little
headland near him, covered with myrtles,
another light twinkled, solitary, dim, and only

just distinguishable. It came from a shrine of the Virgin, and his wandering gaze fixed on it. Suddenly into his dream-world there floated scents of incense, glimmering altars, and sounds of imploring music. ' Star of the sea,' he murmured, ' star of the morning, refuge of sinners, pray for me ! '

Going indoors, he sat down to his desk and wrote his diary of the day's proceedings. Miss Walters filled up a large space in it, and a fragment of what he said about her has been already quoted : but so hard is it to be honest to even a piece of paper, that he made no mention whatever of his qualms of conscience or his own self-accusations.

BOOK II.

CHAPTER I.

WHEN Vernon woke next morning some unlooked-for news awaited him. A fresh, delicious air stole through the open window, and fanned his cheek delicately as he lay thinking. He was enjoying the memory of his last night's adventure, which seemed to promise him a new life in his solitude, when his eye caught something which showed him he had overslept himself. This was a pile of letters on a table by his bedside ; and on top of the pile was one in the handwriting of Campbell. What was his astonishment when he found that it was dated ' Cannes '!

' My dear Vernon,' ran the letter, ' when you see where I am, you will of course set about being angry with me ; and at first sight no doubt I seem to deserve that you should be. A month ago, when you begged me to come abroad and to take a villa with you, I refused you steadily, once or twice a little brusquely ; and this with no better excuse than that very poor one—my feelings. I said I did not feel up to it, and upon my word that was true, Vernon—bitterly, deeply true. I had no heart to travel, and, though you may smile when I say so, the wretchedness I then suffered was crushing me. But I am better now ; life has been going a little more kindly with me. I can enjoy my dinner again some-times; I can laugh at a joke sometimes. My pleasure in my books and pictures is returning to me; and now it has actually happened that you find me abroad as my best chance of happiness. Here I am, doing the very thing by myself that I refused so churlishly to do with you. But I am coming over directly to see you, and make my peace with you; and you will perhaps put me up for a night. You will forgive me, I think, when I tell you all my story.'

Vernon was easily roused into the brightest animal spirits; nor did such sentiment as that of the night previous at all tend to interfere with them. Campbell's letter was like a burst of sunlight to him, and he smiled and whistled in his bath like any happy schoolboy. He immediately telegraphed, 'Come at once. I and my carriage shall fetch you at two o'clock.' He ordered his breakfast in the open air, at his favourite spot under the myrtles; and as he sat there with the liquid morning round him, food, he thought, had never tasted so well, nor nature looked so beautiful.

The friend he was thinking of was a very
different man from himself. What had at
first attracted the two was a certain delicate dilettanteism, and an indifference to the
games and sports by which so many men's
leisure is occupied. But deeper down in
their character this likeness ended. Whereas
Vernon was restless and loved the world,
Campbell was shy and restful and inclined
to solitude ; and whereas Vernon had played
with his affections, Campbell had kept his
laid up in a napkin. There are passions,
however, that lie near affection, although they
are always ready to ruin it ; and to these
Campbell had yielded with a quite sufficient
openness. He had even treated the questions
involved in them with a certain ruthless humour, which was as coarse as that of Rabelais,
and had in part been borrowed from it. But
there had been a flavour of innocence even about
his vices. They had never approached his

heart near enough to corrupt it; and now that at last it was really touched and troubled, he had told the fact to his friend with a simplicity almost childish.

This frankness and depth of feeling had been something of a riddle to Vernon. He had been not long quit of his own engagement when he heard of Campbell's love affair ; and he had pitied his friend sincerely. He looked on him as caught in a trap he had himself just escaped from : and when he found that Campbell the lover interfered with Campbell the friend, the above feeling was intensified. But now as he sat at breakfast, with a volume of Horace beside him, he was happy in the thought that the lover's days were waning, and that the friend would be again restored to him. He had just lit a cigarette, and with a lazy smile was watching the silvery-blue smoke-wreaths as they rose and melted over him into the green myrtle shadows, when he

heard on the gravel the sound of a firm foot-
step, and, looking up, he saw Alic Campbell
before him.

Nothing human could be brighter than a
pleased greeting of Vernon's ; it had all the
quick radiance of a pool in morning sunlight :
and he felt as happy at this moment with his
old friend as a child is with a new plaything.
Campbell, too, for his part was glowing
with glad excitement, though there was a
pathetic tone in his voice, if Vernon had
cared to note it. Campbell was, however,
extremely hungry ; he was by no means indifferent to the minor pleasures of the table,
and Vernon's breakfast was excellent. Food
had the best effect on the lately dejected lover ;
his laugh came gaily, his eye gleamed with
humour. There is many a heartache that
can be made to cease on occasion by the
modest soothings of a good *pâté-de-foie-
gras.*

'Here,' cried Vernon at last, 'are two disciples of Horace; we have tried many philosophies, but we return to this at last.

> Huc vina et unguenta et nimium breves
> Flores amœnæ ferre jube rosæ,
>   Dum res et ætas et Sororum
>   Fila trium patiuntur atra.'

Campbell smiled, and asked for some more Burgundy.

'My dear Alic,' Vernon went on presently, 'I wrote you a letter only yesterday, full of advice and prophecy: and now, strange to say, before you have got either, you have taken the one, and fulfilled the other. I described to you, too, all the charms of this nook of mine; but now, look about you, and enjoy it with your own eyes.'

Campbell looked about him in silent, but evident, admiration. He had been a considerable traveller, and his eyes had known the world's fairest and most famous prospects; but he admitted frankly that till

now he had never seen such a paradise.
Vernon was delighted; and filling a glass
with wine, ' It will be a little island in our
lives,' he said, ' the enchanted time we will
spend here. We have both had our troubles
it is true, but, after all, we are still young :
and it seems to me on a day like this as if
life could have no sorrow except from want of
power to be happy enough. Look between
those two palm trees at the hills with their
misty amethyst. See the astounding blue
above us against the green of the stone-pine !
See how the living azure is cut by the yellow
mimosa-blossom ! The beauty of all this
goes through and through me like some notes
of a violoncello. It is a cry, like certain
dance music, after some consummation of
pleasure unknown to us. You can kiss, you
can embrace a woman; and she can love you
back again. But nature—you can't kiss the
sea; you can't embrace the mountains. If

one could only see God, and break one's
heart in praising Him, that perhaps might
ease one.'

A servant here made a moment's interruption, carrying Campbell's only luggage—
a hand-bag—and asking to know if it should
be taken upstairs to a bedroom. 'Of course,'
said Vernon ; and then turning to Campbell,
'My dear Alic,' he went on, 'it is indeed a
delight to think you are really here. It is a
pleasure beyond hope. But tell me—is that
little bag all you have brought over with
you? You couldn't travel with so little
luggage if you were married.'

'I admit,' said Campbell, smiling, 'that
freedom has its advantages. One would lose
a great deal in losing it.'

'One would lose,' said Vernon, 'all that
makes life bearable, as you would soon have
felt had your affairs gone otherwise. But
about the rest of your luggage, if there's not

a very great deal of it, we might drive over
to Cannes this afternoon, and bring it all
back in the carriage.'

'My dear Vernon,' said Campbell, 'I
have got all I want for the night; and I
must be returning to Cannes to-morrow.
Don't let us waste our one day in driving.'

'Our one day!' exclaimed Vernon. 'God
bless my soul, what do you mean by one
day? Why, you are going to stop here at
least three weeks with me.'

'My dear fellow,' said Campbell very
slowly, 'God knows I should like to stay
with you; but it is not to be.' And he fixed
his eyes upon Vernon with a wistful, serious
tenderness—it might almost be called solemnity. It was quite plain that he was resolute.

This to Vernon was like a thunderbolt
out of a clear sky. He was at once startled,
bewildered, and disappointed.

'Not stay with me!' he exclaimed.

'Why, what on earth do you mean, Alic? Even if you are still a little melancholy, as I can well believe you are, you will be surely far better here than moping about in holes and corners by yourself. Why can't you stay? —tell me?'

When Campbell answered, his voice had almost sunk to a whisper, and he looked at Vernon with eyes that begged for sympathy. 'Because,' he said, 'I have to go on to San Remo. I have to be there to-morrow. Vernon, my—my friend is there. This is the reason why I have come abroad. I may see her to-morrow evening; I think, at farthest, the morning after: and at one time or the other I shall receive my life or death at her hands.'

A sudden unwelcome light at last broke in upon Vernon. '*Her*—her!' he said. 'Why, what on earth are you talking about? It surely can't be true that I have taken your

letter wrongly? I thought, when you told
me your case was mending, that you simply
meant that you had fallen out of love again,
and that you saw that the marriage state
was not a thing worth sighing over.'

Campbell eyed Vernon for a moment or
two with a curious, sad amusement. ' You're
an odd creature,' he at last said, smiling.
' You know something of the world ; at least
you have seen many men and women : and
do you think that a man who has really loved
a woman, can cast his love to the winds in
the course of a single fortnight? What a
strange notion you must have of the nature
of human affection ! '

Vernon, who had not only conceived such
a thing quite possible, but who had in this
case actually taken it for granted, received a
sudden check from those grave words of his
friend. He was not embarrassed by what he
had said himself—he knew Campbell far too

well for that; but he felt that to Campbell's
mind he had betrayed a singular ignorance;
and the first thing that struck him was the
absurdity of his own situation. A look came
into his eyes that fully confessed his fault;
but it was the gleam of humour rather than
a tear of contrition; and his expression was
not unlike that of a naughty child's, who has
been caught for the fifth time committing
some minor mischief. Campbell understood
the expression perfectly; but it neither pained
nor chilled him.

'I don't mind you laughing,' he said.
'True feeling can always stand being laughed
at. Vernon'—and here his own voice sank
low again—'this love of mine has lain down
with me and risen up with me for a whole
year. I have become a new man since first
it took possession of me.'

'So it seems,' said Vernon, 'and a very
much unhappier one.'

'Yes,' said Campbell simply, 'it has made me very miserable. I was ill for several weeks.' His lips quivered a little, and he raised his clear eyes upwards. His look, thought Vernon, was like a young saint's in meditation. Something seemed in his mind which he was a little timid of uttering; but at last he again turned to Vernon. 'I think all this trouble,' he said, 'has been bringing me nearer God.'

Vernon now began to realise that Campbell was really changed. Was this the Campbell who, but a single twelvemonth back, delighted to dwell laughingly on the coarsest side of passion, and used God's name rarely except to give point to an epigram? Vernon saw the change, for he had keen moral perceptions; it oppressed him, and at the same time he respected it. Still, however, a faint hope lingered in him that Campbell might not be beyond repentance. He repeated all the arguments he had before used in his letter, and added others of a more homely and practical nature. 'You have often told me,' he urged, 'about your own circumstances. You are a rich bachelor; you would be a poor husband. I have seen myself that you have always lived in luxury; and you have always travelled whenever the fancy seized you. Marriage would therefore mean to you, on your own showing, the complete loss of all your personal liberty. You would be fettered in every movement and almost in every thought of your life.'

'I know well,' said Campbell, 'all I should have to give up; and I value it as much, or nearly as much, as you do. I should have to give up many, many luxuries, which to me in my self-indulgence have till now seemed necessaries—mental necessaries as well as bodily. I should have to think about all sorts of little expenses—a thing I hate doing.

As you say, my wings would be clipped
for travelling. I could no longer drink the
best Burgundy, or smoke the best cigars, or
buy books with fine engravings in them. I
should lose all this ; but what I should gain
would far—far outweigh it. All this is a
riddle to you, Vernon ; for you have never
known affection.'

'You wouldn't say that, I can tell you,'
replied Vernon, 'if you had seen me last
night.' And he gave a short account, in a
tone of reserved banter, of what he called his
adventure with Miss Walters.

'Adventure !' repeated Campbell. 'Yes
—that is just what you consider a love affair.
With you, it is a little incursion into an
enemy's country ; and your aim is presently to
get back safe again. But when any man loves
truly, does he act or think like this ? Was
it an *adventure* for the Dolorous Mother
when she saw her son die on Calvary ?'

His high-strung state of feeling betrayed itself in every accent; and Vernon at last realised that his friend was beyond his arguments. He put his hand kindly on Campbell's shoulder, and in a tone of compassion that was trying to rise to sympathy, 'My dear, dear fellow,' he said, 'whatever you wish for yourself, I wish. I should be very glad for you to be happy, even though I lost your old *you* by it.'

'Thank you,' said Campbell, smiling; 'but, as time draws on, my hopes get very shadowy. I build only on some slight expression which my friend let drop about me to a third person, and it is more than possible that I quite deceive myself. I feel, in going on to San Remo, as if I were going to my own execution. By this time to-morrow perhaps I shall be the forlornest creature imaginable.'

'And in that case,' said Vernon, 'what

should you do then ? You would come back
to me, wouldn't you, and let me cheer you
up a little? '

Campbell's whole expression altered ; the
lines of his mouth hardened. ' I know exactly
what I should do,' he said. ' I have already
faced the alternative. If necessary, I shall
go straight off to Vienna, and shall find distraction in a complete course of sensuality.
I am told that for a life of pleasure Vienna
is the best of capitals.'

' Nonsense,' said Vernon sharply. ' You
would do nothing of the kind.'

' I should,' replied Campbell. ' I was
never in my life more serious. I have
already settled the exact route I should
travel by, and the hotel I should first put up
at. I am a man of strong animal passions.
I can easily make a complete beast of myself.
Nothing in the world could deaden mental
pain like that.'

'Damn it!' exclaimed Vernon with a sudden angry energy. 'For God's sake, Campbell, do talk like a rational being. It makes me sick to hear you speak in that way. A moment ago I had begun to admire and to envy you; and now you have spoilt all. Because some woman, it chances, does not love you, is that any reason why you should cease to respect yourself? Affection, you say, raises the soul to God; and, for aught I know, it may very possibly do so. But if you are crossed in love, does that make God valueless? Are your views about God dependent on a girl's views about you? If your passion really raises you, it cannot let you plan debasing yourself. If in cold blood you can thus plan debasing yourself, then all I can say is, that I don't think much of your passion.'

'You would not be so hard,' said Campbell meekly, 'if you had ever felt as I feel.

What a lover plans is never in cold blood. Half the vice in the world, Vernon, is caused less by sin than by sorrow. However,' he went on, his tone again softening, ' I didn't come here to croak my woes to you. Let us think about other things, and let us explore your paradise.'

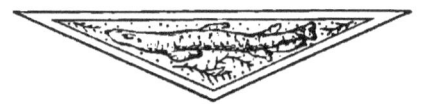

CHAPTER II.

ERNON was charmed to escape to more indifferent subjects, and by a quick reaction Campbell became cheerful. The friends found plenty of small things to amuse and interest them. They went over the villa; they inspected books and etchings; they scrambled about on rocks; they walked through olive-groves; they climbed up a wooded hill, and examined a quaint old chapel. The chapel suggested a sudden thought to Vernon. 'Come,' he said, 'and let us look up Stanley.' The news that Stanley was in the neighbourhood was a fresh distraction for Campbell, and for the

time seemed quite to banish the unfortunate
thoughts that saddened him. Stanley was
living at a small, somewhat rough *pension*,
that was not far from Vernon's villa. They
learnt that he was at home ; and a prim little
white-capped maid left them to announce
themselves. They found him upstairs, in a
small, bare sitting-room, bending over a table,
writing. His face was fine and delicate ; but
had contracted now a slightly stern expression,
and suggested at once thought and physical
suffering. When, however, he saw who were
his visitors, his eyes lit up with a smile of
such frank and surprised pleasure, that for a
moment the sternness vanished ; and Vernon
presently, though not without some mis-
giving, asked him if he would come to
dinner. To his surprise Stanley accepted
gladly ; but added, ' If I come this evening, I
must send you away now ; for I have certain
work which I am obliged to finish to-day.'

'Poor Stanley!' said Vernon, as he and Campbell walked away together. 'How delighted he was to see you, Alic! and I don't think he much minded seeing me.'

'On the contrary,' said Campbell, 'I thought he seemed particularly pleased at it. Why should you think he minded it?'

'I don't know; but I always vaguely fancy, if I haven't wanted to see a man, that he hasn't wanted to see me. Besides, I haven't the least doubt that he thinks me rather a brute.'

'Do you mean to say that's the first time you've ever been to call on him?'

'I'm afraid it is,' said Vernon. 'But I shall go again now. Do you know, it almost made me cry to see the pleased way in which he smiled at us. I am always touched when a man who looks stern is really made glad by a trifle. But I'll tell you, my dear Alic, what our present business must be. We must order

some specially nice things for dinner this evening ; and I think, in spite of everything, we
shall have a very happy little symposium.'

Nor, when dinner came, was this anticipa-
tion falsified. The unlooked-for re-union of
the three old friends produced in each of them
a genial glow of spirits. Stanley, whatever
might be his private habits, betrayed at Vernon's table no trace of asceticism. He was
naturally a moderate man ; but to-night at
least he ate and drank what he wanted, and
in a quite natural way he remarked that the
champagne was good. Talk flowed freely
about the early days at Oxford ; and memory
lit up all of them with the reflected sunshine
of youth. The only one whose spirits were
at all forced or uncertain was Vernon himself.
The thought that Campbell was resolved not
to stay with him vexed him with a suppressed
persistency; and with this presently another
began to mix itself—the thought of Miss

Walters, and the strange charm cf her presence.   It thus happened that at moments
he would appear absent.   But wine came to
his aid whenever his will failed him, and
drove his straying wits back to his guests
and table.

When dinner was over, the three adjourned
to the library, and Stanley and Campbell fell
to discussing one of their college tutors.   This
was a man of great beauty of character, who,
though somewhat rough externally, had had
upon all his pupils the most powerful moral
influence;   and the mention of him led the
talkers to other serious matters.   Vernon at
the beginning had occasionally put in a word
or two ; but he had relapsed gradually into a
mere listener—a listener at first attentive,
then a trifle drowsy ; till at length, by gentle
stages, he had sunk off into sleep.

The tone of the others presently dropped
lower.

'Look!' said Stanley, as his eyes fell upon Vernon, 'what a curious expression in repose he has! He is the most careworn sleeper I ever saw, and yet of all waking men he is the most careless-looking. Do you think he is happy ?'

'He has his troubles,' said Campbell, 'no doubt, like the rest of us. To make him happy, he wants one or two things—he should have less of a heart, or more of one. Somebody, I remember, once said of him bitterly, that he got more love from his slightest friend than he ever gave to his greatest. Perhaps there is some truth in that : and yet, though the man who said it is one of the most staunch of creatures, I could depend on Vernon in some ways more surely than on him. Were there any urgent need, I could ask Vernon to take any trouble for me. He would hate the trouble, yet all the same he would take it; and he would serve you better, when the

service was only a nuisance to him, than
many men would who might feel it a genuine
pleasure.'

'That just fits in,' said Stanley, 'with
what I heard the other day about him, from
an old woman here, whose cottage I sometimes visit. This woman had a poor, lame
child, who was taken out in a mule-cart, with
some of its brothers and sisters. The cart
broke down, and could not be brought home
again ; and the little cripple was naturally in
great distress. Vernon that moment chanced
to be passing by. He at once took it up and
carried it two miles, to its home, and the day
after ordered a boot with steel supports for
it, which the surgeons declare will give it the
use of its legs again. I happened to meet him
just after he had done carrying it, and he said,
" Don't shake hands with me ; I've been
touching a beastly child ! " '

'Have you ever looked at his books ?'

asked Campbell presently, as he glanced round him.

'No; I have never been in this room before. He asked me to breakfast once, but I was unable to come, and I gathered by his manner that he thought he had done his duty by me.'

'His library,' said Campbell, 'made me smile rather. A good half of it consists of dry treatises on theology. Look at his writing-table,' he went on. 'Do you see those three books on it—one on top of the other? I took them up before dinner, and they are " Horace," " The Spiritual Combat," and " Lord Chesterfield's Letters." '

' I remember that at Oxford,' said Stanley, ' he would continually talk of theology ; but it was never with any reverence, though some-times with thought and knowledge.'

'Yes; religion with him,' said Campbell, ' is merely an intellectual question—a tiresome riddle, that piques him because he can't answer it.'

The conversation continued for some time longer, whilst the subject of it still slept heavily. At last Stanley, who kept early hours, declared that he ought to go. 'But I won't wake Vernon,' he said. 'Poor fellow, he looks tired enough. You shall say good-night for me; and I hope, Campbell, that I may soon see you again.'

'I am going to-morrow,' said Campbell. 'I am obliged to go ; but, if you would be in, I might come and see you in the morning. I, too, have my troubles ; and I am afraid I have been boring Vernon with them.'

By and by Vernon woke up with a start, and asked where was Stanley. 'What a brute I must have seemed to him!' he said, when he knew that his guest was gone. 'I ask a fellow to dine with me ; then I sleep like a pig all through the evening ; and now

for my pains, I wake up with a splitting head-
ache. Let us go out—shall we ?—and take
a turn in the garden.'

Vernon was somewhat silent as they went
through the moonlit walks. At last he said
abruptly, ' What made me sleepy to-night was
my having taken too much wine. I did it to
keep my spirits up, for I was gloomy about
your going. Of course Stanley wouldn't say
anything ; but I know quite well he must
have thought me a beast.'

' That,' said Campbell, ' I am quite sure
he did not, for just before he went he
was warmly praising you. He was telling
me of your kindness to some little crippled
girl.'

' My   kindness   to   what ? '   exclaimed
Vernon.   ' Oh, I know what he must be
thinking of.   Poor little dirty brat—she literally reeked of garlic !   How the devil did
Stanley   hear   about   it ?   But   now   tell

me,' he went on, 'must you really go to-morrow ? Is it all quite decided ? Can't you stay even for a day or two, and let me show you my beautiful neighbour ?'

Campbell shook his head. 'No, Vernon —no,' he said.

'But she is very beautiful,' said Vernon, 'and dresses exquisitely, and has all kinds of high-minded views about the hollowness of fashion, and about genuine friendship, and falling in love, and so on. I would let you flirt with her, if you wanted to.'

'You forget,' said Campbell, 'that I am leading a consecrated life.'

'Well, she won't un-consecrate you. She has done with love, she tells me : though I'm not sure myself if I quite believe her. Is it Sterne—or who is it ?—who says, " Talking of love is making it ? " '

Campbell was silent, and Vernon began again.

' I think my true *métier*,' he said, ' would
be that of wooer-in-ordinary to my male
friends. Whenever any one of them had set
his heart on a lady, it should be my business
to awake her love and tenderness ; to teach
her lips to kiss, her breast to move with a sigh
or two, and her eyes to look expressively.
Then without any peculation I would transfer
my complete prize to my client. Would
you on these terms have made me your
agent ? You may be sure when the time
came I should have no temptation to cheat
you.'

This was said with a smile ; but Campbell
answered in a tone of unexpected serious-
ness.

' My dear Vernon,' he said, ' what a
thoroughly immoral man you are !'

' Immoral !'

' Yes ; you really are. I am not in the
least joking. You are one of the most im-

moral men I ever knew. What you said just now is only another proof of it.'

'My dear fellow,' said Vernon, 'I was only chaffing you.'

'Yes; but the man in jest is the key to the man in earnest. Besides, I didn't judge you merely by what you said just now. I have known you for ten years, and have been your friend ever since I knew you. I was looking only this morning at one of your early photographs, and since that was taken I can see how your face has changed. In some ways you have hardly aged at all; you still look very, very young. But youth is sometimes prolonged by a sacrifice of all that is best in it; and ah, Vernon, there is one look gone from your face which that photograph reminded me was once there! And shall I tell you what has destroyed it? It is what I call your immorality. It is this perpetual trifling with your highest and finest

feelings. That the feelings are high and fine
I don't deny for a moment. It is in that
that the badness lies. You are making a
playground of what should be your holy of
holies. You may not be indulging your
grosser appetites ; but you are making yourself incapable for ever of any earnest affection ; and this is the surest way in which you
can quench the Spirit. It is not eclipsing the
light, as lust does ; it is putting the light out.
Pure affection can extinguish lust ; but if you
extinguish pure affection, what then ? Would
a man who has done that ever be fit for
heaven, even though in the world's sense of
the word he were as moral as any an-
chorite ?'

There was something in Campbell's manner which, despite his plain speaking, made
Vernon listen without anger or impatience.
He seemed a little annoyed, however, and
anxious to change the subject.

'Heaven!' he said wearily; 'and do you, Campbell, really believe in heaven?'

'More than you do,' said Campbell, with the same gentleness. 'I am not wanting to preach to you. I am only trying, like a friend that loves you, to show you the reason of your being so ill at ease. This is a delicate thing to do, and even a friend can do it only when he is himself feeling deeply. A year ago I could never have spoken like this to you. Perhaps six weeks hence I shall be again unable to do it.'

'I know you mean kindly,' said Vernon. 'But, honestly, I didn't quite understand you. What on earth makes you think that I am ill at ease?'

'You are, though you may not acknow-ledge it. I can see it in your face, I can hear it in your voice sometimes. With all your bright spirits, and with all your gaiety, you have done your nature a wrong which you feel in spite of yourself. My own sins, God knows, have been many. It is perhaps because of them that all this sorrow is come upon me. But there is something worse, Vernon, than even the garment spotted by the flesh. What is commonly called immorality, does indeed stain life ; but *your* immorality eviscerates it. It leaves you a husk—a shell ; a tissue it may be of supersensitive nerves ; but with no true self within to be informed by them. You have not arrived at that state yet, but there are moments when you feel or fear the beginning of it.'

' I may have causes for care,' said Vernon, 'other than you dream of ; perhaps, indeed, of an exactly opposite nature. You tell me I do not believe in heaven, and perhaps I don't ; but at least I feel daily the want of a belief in it. My unhappiness, if I have any, arises not from having no woman to love, but from having no God to believe in.'

Campbell looked at Vernon with a friendly incredulity. ' My dear Vernon,' he said, ' you are the most irreligious man I know. The same course of conduct that deadens human love deadens divine love also; nor indeed would you play with the first, if you had any real sense of the second. I know quite well that you think about religion, and read about it; but you know quite well also that it is not an active power in your life. It is nothing more than an abstraction. You have continually told me that nothing in life absorbs you, whereas religion, when a reality, is all an affair of loving.'

' Not of loving only, but of believing also. You can't love a being whose existence you are not sure of; and it is quite conceivable —I am not speaking about myself, for that, after all, is a matter of little interest—it is quite conceivable that affection may in many cases be chilled by want of belief, just as belief may become useless for want of proper affection. Love robbed of belief is like a bird whose nest has been stolen. It tries every tree, but finds no twig to rest upon.' There was a short silence after this ; and then presently Vernon began again. ' In one point at least,' he said with a cold laugh, 'you are wrong, Campbell, in your judgment of me. You said that religion had no effect on my life. It was a religious question that caused the breaking off of my marriage.'

' If you had been very much in love, if you had been very anxious to marry, would that question have stood in your way ? '

' It would have stood in my way, I sincerely hope, in any case. I can think of no self-indulgence so wanton, so complete in its cruelty, as bringing children into the world, and giving them no faith to guide them. It would indeed be making a tragic toy of affection, to let it lead one into blowing soap-

bubbles of conscious fretful vanity. Happy
unconscious matter ! The man is worse
than a murderer who informs it with aimless
wretchedness.'

'And this,' said Campbell, 'is the religious
man's view of fatherhood ! My dear Vernon,
you have much to learn yet.'

Vernon made no reply to this. He had
seen that Campbell, in spite of a friend's
fondness, had but a scanty faith in his conduct with regard to the breaking off of his
marriage; and a feeling of not quite unnatural anger had begun to swell up in him.
But 'He means well,' he almost directly said
to himself, and he forced the anger down.
Its only outer sign was a few moments' coldness; and when next he spoke, it was once
more with sympathy.

'You have told me much about love,' he
said, as they moved back to the villa; 'but
you have told me very little about your own

love-story. You met your goddess abroad; she has very simple tastes; "first she would and then she wouldn't," and now she is doubtful whether she will or no. I knew this much, but that is all. Do you mind telling me her name, and a little more about her?'

'Not to-night,' said Campbell. 'No—nor to-morrow morning, I think. Had I better or surer hope, I would dwell on and tell you everything. But I can't now. I can't go over those scenes again. I would sooner not even tell you who she is, unless I can tell you some day that she is or will be my wife. I shall know that soon. Ah, me!'

'And are you still resolved,' said Vernon, 'that Vienna is your only alternative?'

'Perhaps,' said Campbell sighing, 'I am not resolved that it shall be; but I know that it is.'

The conversation then turned to brandy and seltzer-water, and the two friends retired.

CHAPTER III.

CAMPBELL next morning paid a short visit to Stanley, and in the afternoon he was gone. Vernon's last words to him were, ' If you are not successful, come back to me, and give up Vienna. You have told me pretty plainly that I'm not far off from a devil ; so if it's the devil you want to go to, you may at least choose one who is fond of you.'

There was more in his manner, perhaps, than he was altogether conscious of ; for this last farewell of his touched Campbell and set him for some time thinking. As for Vernon

himself, his spirits at first sank low enough, and
his villa looked very blank to him. But he was
not a man tamely to sit down with dejection ;
and, having mourned his friend's loss for an
hour or so, his imagination suddenly wheeled
round to Miss Walters. The effect was as
quick on him as that of a glass of absinthe.
He would at once hurry off and call at the
Château St. John ; and such a thrill did the
prospect send through him, that he felt his
present solitude was not without its advantages. Even a friend like Campbell might
have been perhaps a little *de trop* just then.

He had rung the bell at the Château ; the
hall door had been thrown open, and with a
confident inquiry he was already on the
point of entering, when the servant informed
him that the ladies had left for Nice.

' Left ! ' echoed Vernon in astonishment.

' They left yesterday, sir,' said the servant ;
' but they will be back early this evening, as

I believe they are expecting a gentleman here to dine with them.'

Vernon at once concluded that this gentleman must be himself, and he resolved to hasten home to inquire if no note had arrived for him. He was spared, however, this trouble by the servant adding the next moment, 'A gentleman, I believe, sir, who is coming from Monte Carlo.'

This simple announcement worked like magic on Vernon. A sudden twilight of jealousy fell on his whole soul; and at the same instant the stars of romance shone out again. The expected guest, he felt convinced, could be none other than Colonel Stapleton; and the thought that the beautiful Cynthia could be touched by so gross a rival, seemed to withdraw her to some untold distance. But such are the ways of certain kinds of affection, that this fancied distance only increased his longing for her. His impressions of her, mental or sensuous, became all more vivid than ever, and he was soon lost in a deep, passionate reverie. Her eyes, her lips, her hands, the texture of her cheek and throat, the feather in her hat, the tones of her voice, her gestures—all these in their several ways touched him ; and she dwelt in his mind as some strange, delicate mystery that he was resolved to make his own.

Having indulged to the full in this kind of dreaming, the thought of Campbell once more came back to him. He paced the same walks that evening that Campbell had lately paced with him ; and he attentively thought over their last night's conversation, and looked longingly in the direction of the Château St. John. ' Ah me ! ' he cried, ' and am I really the brute that Campbell tells me I. am ? Am I really heartless and selfish, and with no health left in me ? '

He went indoors to his library ; and took

down a volume from his book-case of Latin
authors. He sat for some time poring over it
motionless; but at last a low voice broke
from him, and he began thus translating aloud
to himself :—

'Highest and holiest, mightiest and al-
mightiest, most pitiful and yet most just, un-
seen and yet ever near to us, fairest and yet
most firm, ever before us and yet past our
studying; never new, never aging, yet renew-
ing all things ; striking the proud with age,
and they know it not: whose work never
ceases, whose quiet is never broken;
gathering, yet nothing needing ; sustaining,
replenishing, and protecting ; making, cherish-
ing, and maturing ; seeking, yet having all
things: Thou lovest, and passion stirs Thee
not ; Thou art jealous, and lo! no care
touches Thee ; Thou repentest Thee, yet
Thou has no contrition ; Thou art angry, and
yet Thou abidest calm ; Thou makest Thy

works change, but Thy counsel endures for
ever ; Thou findest what Thou hast never
lost, and Thou takest it back home to Thee.
Thou art never in want, and yet Thou art
pleased with winning ; Thou hast no covet-
ousness, and yet Thou takest usury.   Thou
art paid more than Thy due that Thou mayest
be made man's debtor ; and who has aught
that has not been always Thine ?   Thou
payest, yet owest no man anything ; Thou
givest gifts, and behold Thou losest nothing.
And what, oh, what is this that I say concerning Thee, my God, my life, my holy and
sweet desire ? or what, when he speaks of
Thee, can be said by any man ? and yet woe
to him that speaks not, since even the dumb
praise Thee.'[1]

The book over which Vernon was bending
was the ' Confessions of Augustine.'   As he
read he felt his eyes moisten, and at last he

---

[1] *St. Augustine's Confessions*, book i. chap. iv.

started at a tear that dropped on the page before him.

'What's Hecuba to me, or I to Hecuba?' he exclaimed. 'Do I really mean that? or is it only another form of self-indulgence? My God, what am I? Is there anything in me not contemptible?'

He hid his face in his hands, and remained for some time motionless. When he moved himself, he did so with resolution. He opened a drawer in his writing-table, he took out some paper, and after a certain further hesitation he abruptly put pen to it.

What he wrote was as follows :—

'Why should a man wince at the sight of his inmost thoughts? Is he not a coward, if he does not dare confront them? Ah me! I am a coward; I wince and I hold back; false shame overcomes me. But my heart is troubled; my spirit is bruised and beaten, and courage at last has come to me from my

wretchedness.   I may pretend I am happy;
but, O my God, I am not happy !   It is true
that my friends or the delicious sunshine
make my blood beat with pleasure, and many
other such trifles excite me.   I become ex-
cited childishly; and I forget myself into a
bright false happiness.   But all the while
there is a worm gnawing at my heart, and
whenever I am quiet I feel it.   I have tried to
deceive myself; I have tried to say this is not
so.   But I can deceive myself no longer;
and now I will face the truth.   I will see
what I am ; I will examine this mangled self
of mine.   Yes—I will put my thoughts into
shameless black and white ; they shall have
a solid body that I cannot pretend eludes
me.   Quick !—though I am shuddering, let
me get the icy shock over; let me plunge
into confession.   What should make me hesi-
tate ?   No one will see these pages, with this
blurred image of my soul cast on them.

Whenever I wish it the fire can keep my secret.

'What shall I say? Shall I speak as in reality my soul pines to speak? I will.

'O my God, holiest and mightiest, most pitiful and yet most just, what I pine for is to speak to Thee. Let me write Thy name— let me brand it in writing, not think it only in faint and fleeting thoughts. Let me rouse my ears with the sound of my own voice cry- ing to Thee. O God, what I long for is to lay bare my soul—to open it, to disrobe it, to expose it naked before Thee; and to cry to Thee to have pity, to have pity, and to look upon me!

' And yet, how dare I, impure and faith- less, loving nothing—so they tell me—and nobody? For Thou art pure and holy; and my very friend has told me that I am viler than most men. Am I so? Oh, teach me to know myself; humble my

pride; enlighten me! My God, I am not
mocking Thee. What I ask of Thee is what
my heart is crying for. Teach me to know
myself.

'And yet if indeed Thou hearest me, I
must seem like one mocking; for Thou
knowest how faith has failed me, and how
bewildered and dark my mind is. Even
whilst I am crying to Thee, whilst I am trying to open to Thee all my secret being, I
know not, I am not sure, if you have any
existence—you, the God I am crying to.
Perhaps you are only a dream—an idea—a
passing phenomenon in man's mental history.
And yet surely, if Thou existest, Thou wilt
not, even for this cause, turn away from me,
quenching the smoking flax. May it not
be that Thou art revealing Thyself to
me, through my wretched sense of Thy
absence?

'But from me why art Thou absent? Is

it through my sins, through my own loveless
nature? Have I nothing in my soul fit to
offer Thee? And for this cause hast Thou
put me far away from Thee?

'I may be evil now; I may be in outer
darkness; but I know that I was not always.
I was once near Thee; I was once ever with
Thee. That was when I was a little child.
O my God, I will confess to Thee through
my childhood.

'I was no saint, Thou knowest; I was a
little, worldly child, yet I will maintain even
to Thy face that as a child I loved Thee, and
with a child's frankness I was always in secret
turning to Thee. I thought of Thee in my
play; I thought of Thee in riding my pony.
Hardly an hour passed in which, without
kneeling, I did not say some word to Thee.
Nor did this end with my childhood; for as I
grew older, and as my thoughts multiplied,
more and more in secret did they fasten upon

Thee. And I grew very greatly to fear Thee, and yet I was not afraid to love Thee ; for my own sins were small, and I washed them out with nightly penitence. Often hast Thou heard my childlike lips confessing them.

'But as I thought upon Thy perfections, and as I looked round upon the world, a new sense grew in me. It was a sense of the world's sin, and of how Thou wast being grieved and blasphemed everywhere. Of men's sorrow, and want, and poverty, I had not heard much. What touched me was the misery of the sin that they lay wallowing in. The thought of this was never quite absent from me. It haunted me day and night through all my later boyhood. It very often subdued me in my gayest moments. Thou knowest how for this reason a great city was hateful to me. In the same way, although I could see my schoolfellows unhappy, and be little moved by it, yet many a time when I have seen some young soul corrupting itself, I have said, " I would die, if he might be saved from sinning." O God, Thou hast heard me, if Thou hearest anything. Thou knowest, too, how my pillow has been damp with tears from my thinking on these things.

'Thus the time drew on when there was a new thing to happen to me. I was to draw near to Thee at Thy Son's altar. For this cause, I turned my thoughts upon myself more earnestly; and I cleansed my heart as I had never done before. And I received Thy Son's self into me with fear and trembling; and I was drawn closer, O Thou Holy One, to Him and Thee. And at the same time also my early life was expanding. My passions and the world's excitements began to stir me, and shot new colours into existence; and I hoped for love and for com-

panionship, and I longed for beauty. The
sadness and the rapture overcame me that
together stir men to singing. But Thou, O
my God, wert present in all this. If I longed
for the love of a woman, it was that both our
faces might turn to Thee. And I saw Thee,
too, in the blue sky and in the sunset, and in
the reedy river with the moon in it, and in
the sea, and the sea-shore. And each year I
was tempted with more and more temptations,
but I still kept watch over myself, and always
in my trouble I cried to Thee. I spoke to
no friend about these things. I communed
with Thee only, and I tried very hard to
carry the cross of Christ. When I have been
dining with gay companions I have seen
His face before me, beyond the lights and
glasses. I have seen Him worn and sorrow-
ful, pleading with and reproaching me. He
has often said to me in the midst of my
laughter, " I have suffered so much for thy

sake, canst thou not suffer even a little for Mine ? "

' I lived like this for some four or, it might be, five years, and then the time began when Thou wert slowly to be withdrawn from me. Why was this, my God ? Was it for my sins ? And if so, for what sins ? When, when did they begin ? For Thou wast not withdrawn from me through my forgetting Thee, but through my ever thinking of Thee. I studied much and many things; and whatever I studied, I applied it to Thy Church and Thee. And new lights broke on me, and new roads of knowledge ; and my soul suffered violence, and the sight of its eyes was changed. For by-and-by, though the change came very slowly, all that I had once been taught about Thee, the Sacraments also, through which I once thought I approached Thee, became to me like outworn symbols. I struggled to stay the change. I called to

Thee, Thou knowest how often, to keep it from me. Thou knowest how, as I felt my prayers grow faint, and their words lose their meaning, I still said to Thee every night and morning, " I believe ; help Thou mine unbelief." Thou knowest, too, when Thou gavest me no answer, how I tried to find help thus, " He that doeth," I said, " shall know of the doctrine ; " and I tried with fresh diligence to do my daily duties, hoping that in this way might my faith revive again. But it never did revive. On the contrary, all this while I was receding farther from Thee ; and the more earnestly I sought Thee, the less near did I seem to come to Thee, till at last I was like a blinded bird, I knew not whither even to try to fly; and this body of mine, this Temple of Thy Holy Spirit, has been left empty ; and vain thoughts and desires had been holding and still hold festival in it.

'O my God, if Thou art, why for me art Thou not? Why art Thou thus withdrawn from me? Is it because I have sinned? Can that be the reason? Surely this Thou knowest, that it was not what men call sin that made my eyes dim to see Thee. It was not the lust of the flesh, nor the pride of life, although both of these assailed me. And if since then evil things have had hold on me, I have sinned because I first lost Thee; I have not lost Thee through sinning. There is no man or woman that for Thy sake I could not renounce easily, reserving no more care for them than to work for their souls indifferently. No—what I have lost Thee by is not sin; it is rather the very things whereby I resisted sin; it is my reason, my intellect, and my longing for what is true. I have lost Thee, my God, through my earnest search to find Thee.

'And yet, for all this, do I dare to say I

am sinless ? It may be that I am far worse
than I think I am ; for has not my very friend
told me that I am viler than most men ?
Does he speak truth ? Perhaps. For in
many ways—it may be in all ways—he is a
better man than I am. The ties and the
affections of this life—those joys and sorrows
with which Thou hast surrounded us—touch
him, and take hold of him, and leave deep
marks in him ; but me they touch only as
the shadows in a dream-night. Perhaps, then,
here is the secret. Perhaps I am vile, not
knowing it, because to renounce all for Thy
sake would be so very small a pang to me,
and a sacrifice to Thee is worthless of that
which costs us nothing. What then ? Must
one love Thy creatures before one can love
Thee ? Must one not rather love Thy
creatures because of Thee ?

' Thy creatures ! Were they Thine I
could indeed love them. I should know that

there was in them some eternal worth and value. But, without Thee, what are they more than shadows are? What are they more than I, who am the most frail and vain of shadows? They get no hold on me, nor I any on them. For a little while one pleases me, and then a little while and it does not please. It comes near me; presently it recedes again, and another is pushed into the place of it; and in me there is left no regret, nor any pain in my heart. And how shall this be otherwise? And what shall give these ghosts substance? Why, without Thee, what but a mere ghost is the universe, even to its farthest stars? Of the only cosmos man can ever know or conceive of, he is himself the co-creator; and with the ending of his consciousness the All ends also. It falls like a house of cards when one card is taken away from it. Such is it without Thee. And yet it is told me that if I loved my fellow-ghosts, above all if I would take to my heart some one of them, they would then be ghosts no longer; and that, they being thus made real to me, I should again discern Thee.

' This may be true. There may be some philosophy in it. By Love as well as by the Word, the Heavens are perhaps made. But, O my God, wouldst Thou only reveal Thyself first to me, wouldst Thou only show me that Thou indeed existest, I would love all things then for Thy sake!

' And yet should I ? I am not certain of that even. For, my God, if Thou existest Thou lovest all Thy creatures, and they are all infinitely precious. How, then, am I to inflame or influence my heart, that I should permanently love some one of these more than I love the others ? I am perplexed, I cannot tell. Yet I know—even my common sense tells me—that it is only in this way that loving men do love.

'Nay, this, too, Thou knowest of me, that I have, as a fact, striven to love in this way. I sought to marry, and to be faithful all my life to another; and I trusted that with another's eyes I might again discern Thee. But even this hope failed me. For what return did she whom I chose make to me? She gave me no help that I needed; but proffered me comfortless comfort, and help that I had no need of. Instead of showing me *Thee*, she turned away and prepared to worship *me*. She would have made me into *her* God, instead of guiding me to *mine*. And for a time this consoled me a little; but I soon grew weary of it, and more restless than ever. For how should this blind passion satisfy me? I did but blind her to Thee. She did not show Thee to me.

'It seems, then, that I have tried everything. And now, my God, what remains for me? How shall I plant my foot firm in this

land of shadows ? I am not in pain. Ah,
if I were in pain there would be more hope
for me ! I would not complain to Thee that
I did not feed upon roses, if Thou wouldst
vouchsafe only that the thorns might wound
and tear me. And yet, O God, Thou knowest I am distracted still by trifles, by pleasures
that are no pleasures, and by pains that are
no pains. And Thou hast given me high
spirits, and Thou hast hidden my soul in a
raiment of light laughter, and in what, even
to me, sometimes seems contentment. But
my brain is empty ; I know not where to
turn. To this thing and to this thing I would
apply myself; but whenever I begin to stir
myself, the reason which Thou hast given me
plucks me by the ear, and hisses in a whisper,
" To what purpose ? Are not all things
vanity ? "

    ' And what is this I say ? To whom am
I speaking ? I am speaking to One of whose

very existence I am doubtful. I am not certain if I would stake a hundred pounds upon
it. Oh, my forlorn hopes! My reason trips
me, I am entangled and thrown down. Fool
that I am—wretched, wretched fool! And
yet, though I am thus lying prostrate, thrown
abject and confused upon the ground, I will
not be hindered. O God, I still will speak
to Thee. I will call Thee to witness that
at least I *have* been near Thee, that I *have*
known Thy presence, and that, far away
though I be from Thee now, though this
world of shadows may now blind my eyes
to Thee, there nothing is in it anywhere
that I have longed for as I have longed
for Thee, there is nothing I have desired in
comparison of Thee. Thou hast been to me
my all, my life, my light, and my salvation.
Thou hast been the one wealth of my soul—
its one and only fire; and all that has hidden
Thee has been but as burning ashes.

'Am I mad? Am I a hypocrite? Am
I dreaming? Am I lying to myself, as I
write thus? Am I playing a part before
myself to deceive myself? O my God, after
all, is it nothing but my own sin, my own
lovelessness, that stands between me and
Thee? Dost Thou put me away, seeing
how lightly I have esteemed Thy creatures?
Have I, as Campbell said to me, quenched
Thy Spirit?

'How odd Campbell's name looked, stuck
in like that!

'My God—is it not possible that I may
plead my cause thus with Thee? May I not
justify myself to Thee, and say, the worse I
am now, the more does this show how I loved
Thee? Thou wast present in every affection,
in every energy of my life; therefore with
Thy withdrawal every energy, every affection
is ruined. Yes—I might say this, but for one
thing. Ah me, my God, behold what is now

happening to me! The desire of Thee has long made me miserable; and, ah, more miserable that I am! even my desire for Thee is now deserting me. My heart is ceasing to ache for Thee. A hateful peace is slowly soothing it to its death. My soul is getting colder and colder; warmth is leaving it, as it leaves a man who is dying. O my God, remain with me! Keep my pain and my desolation alive in me! If Thou wilt not fill the void in my heart that Thou didst once fill, let the void remain void, let nothing else fill it. Give me no peace, unless it be Thy peace. Torment me, but forsake me not. Scourge me, keep me wretched and restless till I find Thee! This is indeed a sincere prayer. O my God, is it a wrong one?'

Here he came to a long pause, and threw his pen down, as if he would write no more. He looked round the room wearily, and

stared in a kind of stupor at the various
books about him. At last his eye fixed on a
volume of Herbert Spencer ; and for many
minutes he was motionless. Then, seizing
the pen again, he rapidly added what follows.

'Our own inward condition—our own sins
and longings, and the bitter strife between
them—to the teachers of the present day
what trifles do such things seem !—or at best,
what a storm in a saucer ! To the prophets
of humanity, an unskilful bricklayer is a
more tragic object than a ruined soul !'

Several times during the long course of
his writing, Vernon had gone to the window,
and peered out. He now went again once
more, and the moon was setting—the moon,
which during his after-dinner walk had been
so high in the middle heavens. This showed
him that the night must be far spent. Presently his eye fell on a small side-table, and
there lay an object so common-place that it

seemed to him like a spectre. It was a letter
he had not before noticed that had come for
him by the evening's post. The writing,
which was large and decided, might have
been either a man's or woman's ; and he
fancied it was familiar, though he could
connect no name with it. He broke open
the envelope, as if the sight of it half
dazed him ; and the first words he read sent
all the blood to his cheek.

'Dear Mr. Vernon,'—began the letter,
'When I saw you the other day, I quite forgot
to tell you that my very heart was broken.
('What!' thought Vernon, 'can this be from
Miss Walters?' He went on reading.)
'And only a clever young man like you
can be of the least comfort to me. My poor
little darling sky-terrier Prinny—the thing
on this earth I have loved best and longest
—was run over and killed the other day by a
young man with a tandem. Only conceive

it—a tandem! And this young gentleman
could have hardly held in a donkey. Had
he been one of my own stable-helps, I should
have known pretty well what to do with him.
And now you—if you will, I want you to
write an epitaph for me. My angel is being
embalmed by a very accomplished bird-
stuffer, and is to have Christian burial when
I get back to England. Your verses shall
have a most honourable place; so be a good
man, do, and write them for me.' And
then followed the bold signature of the
Duchess.

With a tired, sleepy smile Vernon again
sat down at his writing-table. A thought
had struck him suddenly; and seizing the
pen, he scribbled these hasty lines:—

Thou art gone to sleep, and we—
May we some day sleep like thee!
Prinny, were this heart of mine
Half so true, my dog, as thine,
I my weary watch should keep
For a something more than sleep!

Whatever besides sleep the exhausted writer may have longed for, sleep, at least, now unexpectedly fell upon him. His eyelids grew heavy like lead, the pen dropped from his hand, and, sinking back in his chair, he became lost to consciousness.

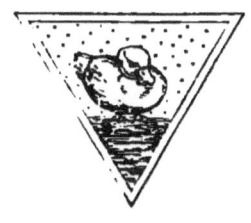

BOOK III.

CHAPTER I.

WHEN Vernon awoke it was already daylight: the Venetian shutters were barred with the red gleams of morning. His eyelids ached, and he looked about him bewildered.

'What has happened to me?' he said to himself. 'Am I awake, or is this a nightmare?'

He paced about the library, at first almost staggering; but by-and-by he recovered himself. He mounted to his bedroom. It had a ghastly, alien aspect. There was his bed, cold, smooth, and unslept in, with his night-

shirt folded lying upon it. He ruffled the
sheets and pillow, that he might seem to his
servant to have passed the night as usual ;
for, as to lying down, it was the last thing he
now thought of. Then he tore his clothes
off and plunged into a cold bath. He re-
dressed himself ; he made a large cup of coffee over a spirit-lamp; and having drunk it,
he softly stole out of doors.

The long shadows of the clear day in its
infancy made his garden wear an unfamiliar
face for him. But the living breath of the
air, fresh with the dew, and quick with the
smells of flower-beds, woke in him new pulses.
He paused and looked about him that his
spirit might 'drink the spectacle.'[1] The sea
was a pale sheet, sharply dark at the horizon,
where it washed with its long levels the red-
dening tract of sunrise ; and it was strewn

---

[1]   His spirit drank
The Spectacle.—WORDSWORTH.

with floating fragments of the crocus and the rose of the sky. The faint promontories of Italy slept in a veil of vapour. Inland lay the far hill-villages, white scattered specks on the huge slopes of the mountains ; and below them were sombre ranges of far-reaching mounded olive-woods. These were unchanging in their soft, impassive darkness ; but except on these the light was brightening everywhere : and presently, far beyond them, all the gigantic highlands flushed in an instant from grey to a shining rose-colour, as they caught the risen splendour on their bleak frosts or dews.

Vernon, as he looked, felt himself come to life again, but to a life of clear sensation rather than clear thought. Thoughts, however, of some kind must have begun to dimly stir in him ; for he soon found himself moving in a definite direction. It was the direction of the Château St. John. He passed through a wicket, into a large open expanse studded with heath and furze-bushes. The sea was on one side of it ; it was traversed by several paths ; and, for the sake of the air and view, he had often before wandered in it. Here he paused. Beyond were the tufts and plumes of the luxuriant Château shrubberies, and between these, by glimpses, the Château itself was visible. Vernon's eye fixed on the line of windows. The blinds were down ; the whole house seemed slumbering. The path where he stood led to a marble gateway, through which one entered the gardens and passed into an avenue of orange-trees. Towards this gateway, though he could not explain why, he was, in another moment, moving. Last night he could write his thoughts ; now they were too vague for analysis.

He passed through the gates with a feel- ing of hope and peril ; he might have been entering the charmed bounds of a sorceress.

And yet the place was already known by heart to him ; and only a week ago he had roamed at his own will in it. A maze of paths branched from the orange-avenue. He instinctively chose one that led far away from the house, and that brought him by-and-by to a long succession of gardens, terraced on the hill-side, and leading down to the sea. He stole on rapidly, past urns and statues, fountains and set flower-beds; he descended by broad flights of steps from one level to another ; and he at last diverged into a steep winding path, which dived into a natural tunnel amongst certain fantastic rocks. This brought him presently, after several turnings, to the strand of a tiny bay. On either side was a curve of sheltering cliffs, not lofty but precipitous, and plunging straight into clear grey-green sea-water. The strand was a little platform, gravelled carefully, and backed by a bed of violets.

Here he paused, and at last began to meditate. Slowly his vague feelings turned into thoughts and images. His vigils of the night came back to him, with the strange projection on paper he had made of his own condition : and they took a ghastly aspect as the air of the morning breathed on them. Mixed, too, with these phantasmal memories were thoughts of a different order, which soon began to reveal themselves with semi-transparent bodies. They were thoughts of the clear-cheeked mistress of the grounds where he was now trespassing. No sooner had he become conscious of this, than a memory came back to him of certain sayings of Campbell's ; and he exclaimed to himself, with weary self-reproach, ' Do I think again of yielding ? What is it that has brought me here ? I do not love this girl. I have no wish to bind myself. All the fine and all the high feelings she stirs in me—they are not

serious : I attach no worthy meaning to them.
I am merely trifling with them in the very
way Campbell warned me of. Let me be
brave for once—let me make one sacrifice ;
let me call my imagination away from her.
And yet—ah me—those lovely, lovely lips ot
hers !'

At this moment a slight noise startled
him. He turned quickly round, and there, at
the distance of a pace or two, she was herself
standing before him. In an instant, like bats
from daylight, his scruples took wing, and hid
themselves. He was conscious of a shock, as
of all his will yielding. For a little while he
stood silent and looked at her, feeling nothing
but his own blood beating, and letting his
eyes rest on her. Seen thus in the dawning
she was a fresh surprise to him. His
memory, it is true, had retained her image
clearly ; but it had let the image tarnish, and
lose its exquisite delicacy. He saw she was

far more lovely than in his thoughts just now
she had seemed to him. She was dressed in
a way that, it was evident, was meant only
for solitude. She had a long cloak on, with
a border of broad sable. It was fastened
round her throat, with additional closeness, by
a small brooch of diamonds; and below it
descended a pale-blue satin dressing-gown.
She had apparently taken what at waking
she could first seize upon; for on her slim
shoes there was a glimmer of gold em-
broidery, and on one of her hands was a long
evening glove. The other was bare, and
held a pale, dewy rose in it.

Vernon's rapid glance took in all these
details; and the same impression was renewed in him that he received at first meeting
her. Everything about her was dainty,
almost *fine* in its daintiness; yet, in relation
to her, it seemed natural as her own complexion. And she herself, with the early

light caressing her—had that complexion
stolen a tint from morning ? Had the dews
of night washed her violet eyes clearer ?

Miss Walters was the first to speak ; but
she only exclaimed, ' Mr. Vernon ! ' and he
for the first moment could only exclaim,
' Miss Walters ! ' He was not, however, a
man to remain long tongue-tied ; and very
soon, with a smile, he was begging pardon as
a trespasser. ' Before you came here,' he
said, ' these gardens were a favourite haunt
of mine ; and I thought that, under cover of
the morning, I might venture in, just once
more, undetected.'

' And I thought,' said Miss Walters, with
a glance at her own costume, ' that I might
be undetected also. I certainly did not come
out expecting to confront company.'

The soft, low voice in which these words
were murmured, showed Vernon that she was
not displeased at meeting him. Directly

afterwards she happened to drop her glove. She
fixed her eyes on him smiling, and said, ' Pick
that up, will you ? '   It was a simple request to
make, but it had in it that subtle note of command, the assumption of which by a woman
is one of the first signs of an understanding.
Vernon realised this perfectly, and his
heart swelled with rapture. He was fully
launched now on the tide of luxurious feeling;
and he murmured secretly, as his eyes met
his companion's, ' My own ! my own !' The
consciousness of having even in thought
applied such a phrase as this to a woman,
might be to many men a sharp self-revelation ;
but Vernon knew himself far too well
for that. No lover, however, of the most
earnest and genuine kind could have put
more tender expression than he did into his
voice, when he asked her presently, 'Are
you always so early a riser as this ? '

' No,' she said; 'but I slept badly last

night ; and the morning looked so beautiful.
I huddled on these things, as you see—
anything I could get together ; I stole out
noiselessly, and found myself in a fairy-land
of roses, silent and fresh with dew. I hardly
know these gardens yet. They are all a
wonder and delight to me. I had never ex-
plored that little tunnel before ; and you may
judge how surprised I was when I found you
standing here.'

'Let me show you,' said Vernon, 'the
mysteries of your own domains. Let us go up
again, and I will be your *valet de place.*'

She turned, and she went with him. His
whole being was possessed with the sense of
her near companionship. They wandered on
together through the more sequestered walks,
slowly and often pausing, for the sake of
some sight or sound. Now it was a bird's
song that arrested them, now a prospect—a
fan-palm, an arch of roses, or the peaks of

the distant Alps : and such things as these
were for some time all they talked about.
Impersonal, however, as the conversation
seemed to be, a sense of mutual ease between
them was growing under its kindly shelter ; nor
was this to be wondered at.   Conversations
which are impersonal in form, are sometimes
intensely personal in spirit.   The subjects
spoken about are like the masques worn at
a ball ; and a passion can be declared plainly
under the guise of praising a view.   Things
on the present occasion had not come to this :
but the conversation was full, on both sides, of
oblique hints of feeling ; and the subtle response of Miss Walters to every sight of
beauty revealed to Vernon new depths in her
character.   She saw a thousand minute things
that his eyes had passed over, even to the
play of the dewdrops falling from leaf to leaf ;
and when he pointed out to her the wider
and bolder prospects, the feelings they stirred

in her seemed to be more deep than his own.
She looked, he thought, amongst the dews
and the roses, like the spirit of the morning
facing its own creations.

Presently he was preparing to turn up a
certain path, when with a quick movement
she put her hand on his arm, and stopped
him. 'Not that path,' she said. 'It brings
us in full view of the house; and to the
observation of the servants, I think, we should
be a somewhat mysterious couple.'

When a woman once shows herself conscious that she is doing anything clandestine, a
man can rarely avoid some slight change in his
manner towards her; and Vernon now, as
they diverged into a different path, felt that
he turned to her with a slightly less disguised
admiration. Any such freedom, however,
spent itself like a relapsing wave, as his look
encountered hers. Hers showed no fear

of, or no offence at, him. It was full only
of a sad, earnest inquiry, as though she were
wondering what were his feelings. As she
thus regarded him, she betrayed something
he had not before noticed. In spite of its
radiant aspect her face bore signs of weari-
ness, and under her eyes were streaks of
transparent purple.

'Yes,' she said absently, as Vernon remarked on this; 'last night I was very wake-
ful. And you,' she added—'I think the same
fate must have been yours. Why, Mr.
Vernon, how is it that this has escaped me ?
You are more than tired; haggard is the
only word for it. Has anything painful
happened to you ?'

Vernon was silent for a few moments;
then he answered smiling, 'You make me
speak to you; your voice acts like a spell on
me. I spent last night face to face with a
spectre. I spent it face to face with that

dead self of mine which I told you I had come here to find again.'

'Yes,' she said; 'you told me. To some people your words might perhaps have had no meaning. But I understood them. I have seen and known things that made them quite plain to me. Tell me, then—have you so soon found what you were seeking for?'

'Not it—no; but the phantom of it. It was the piteous phantom, not the returning friend. At least I think so; for just now I can be sure of nothing. Some day, perhaps, I may be able to tell you better.'

'I, too,' she said, 'have something that I may perhaps tell *you*—some day.'

Vernon was silent for a moment; and then he said to her, 'Give me that rose as a pledge that you will keep your promise.'

'It is not a *promise*,' she murmured; 'it is a *perhaps* only.' But at the same time with

a slow, regretful movement she gave him
the pledge he asked for.   As he took the
flower from her, their hands touched; for a
few seconds they lingered in light contact,
and then gently, and with no resistance on
her part, Vernon took hers in his own.   As
he held it, he looked into her face silently;
by a slight movement he made her turn round
to the sunrise, and raising the rose in his
hand, he laid it against her cheek.   'And you
are pale,' he said, 'like one of these creamy
rose-petals.   See what you have given me—
it is your own image.'

Miss Walters made no answer, excepting
with her eyes and with her cheeks, whose
living rose-leaf flushed with a faint carnation.
A pause here might have been not without
embarrassment.   Vernon felt this with the
instinct of the true love-maker, and he lit on
a new subject instantly.   He saw that in her
left hand she was holding a small volume,

and with a voice quite altered, he asked,
' What have you got there ? '

'You would hardly guess perhaps,' she
said, with a little, flickering smile. 'It is a
Bible. I always keep it by the side of my
bed, and I always read a verse or two in
the morning when I get up. I make my
selections in a way no critic would approve
of ; and I'm sure I can't explain to you what
my exact principle is. This morning I chose
—shall I tell you what ? Let us sit down
upon this bench for a moment, and I will read
it out to you. No—' she said, putting her
hand on his, ' you must not take the book
from me. I don't want you to see the con-
text. " Awake, O north wind ; and come,
thou south ; blow upon my garden, that the
spices thereof may flow out. . . . I sleep, but
my heart waketh : it is the voice of my
beloved that knocketh, saying, Open to me,
my sister, my love, my dove, my undefiled :

for my head is filled with dew, and my locks with the drops of the night." '

The selection of this passage was a slight shock to Vernon, or rather the fact that, having selected it, she should have thus read it to him. But so absent from her seemed all consciousness that it could have any personal application, that he instantly felt ashamed of so vulgar a suspicion of her.

' They are beautiful verses,' he said, ' and you read them beautifully. I am going to ask you an odd question, seeing that this is only our second meeting. Do you say prayers in the morning, as well as read the Bible ? '

' I am a person,' she said abstractedly, ' who has said many prayers—many, many, many. I have passed nights of watching, just as last night you did. But women endure and suffer with more patience than men do.'

'With more patience, yes; because they have less to suffer.'

'Do you think that is true?' she said, smiling sadly.

'Not of all women—no; but of women like you it must be. The sufferings we talk of are those of the heart and spirit. I don't know your history; your burdens may have been more heavy than mine; but they have been burdens of a nobler kind; they have been such as are laid only on those who are fit to bear them. It is far easier for the saint to carry the cross, than for the sinner to find or raise it again when he has once dropped it in the snow.'

Again she looked at him with the same sad smile. 'Do you think,' she said, 'that I am a saint, then?'

'No,' he answered; 'you are not a saint. But I think you are listening for the sounds that the saints hear.'

Presently he resumed. ' I might perhaps have thought you were a saint already, if it were not for one reason.'

' And what reason is that ? '

' Do I venture to tell you, I wonder ? It is entirely a subjective reason. Well—it is this. If I knew that you would never know it, or that, knowing, you would forgive or forget it, I feel quite sure that I should touch your lips with mine.'

As Vernon said this, he again put out his hand to her, but, instead of meeting it, she raised hers to her face, and for a moment hid her eyes with it.

' Remember,' she said presently, ' nothing like that must ever come into our friendship. I have set you apart in my own mind from all other men, and you must learn to think of me not as others have done.' She seemed to be half pleading with and half warning him ; and her words came with a singular soft solemnity which at once fanned his feelings and made him resolved to check them. 'You must think of me,' she went on, 'just as I am to think of you. I am your friend, or, if you like it, your sister : and near relations, you know, are only absurd when they are sentimental.'

Vernon could not understand her. She was evidently all in earnest ; but there was something in herself, some subtle power in her presence, by which her words were more than neutralised. 'Surely,' he thought, 'this is not the voice of a sister; and when feelings are merely sisterly, it is never worth while saying so.' He was stung by a hybrid impulse—the wish to obey her words and the wish to yield to her fascination.

'I will think of you,' he exclaimed, 'in any way you tell me to : and you shall let me call you by the name you have yourself taught me—my sister, my love, my dove, my undefiled. May I call you that ?'

She made no answer, but she clasped her hands before her; he could see that she clasped them tightly : and she sat motionless with her eyes turned upwards. At last she said, ' Could you only call me that truly, I would give up everything ! '

' What,' murmured Vernon, ' should hinder me ? My love, my dove, my undefiled, I shall always connect you with the clear dews of the morning; and your friendship will revive my life like a second baptism.'

' You are reckoning without your host,' she answered, still looking straight before her. ' You know nothing about me yet, nor who it is you are speaking to.'

' What is wanting in my knowledge,' said Vernon, ' is made up by my instincts. Think, we have only met twice; and yet already you are my friend and my sister, and you have already—at least, I think so—put a new life into me. I feel like a dusty flower that has had dew fallen on it.'

She rose from where they were sitting, and began to walk on slowly. He followed her in silence, watching her graceful movements. A long branch of roses dangled across the path. She drew it towards herself, and stood still, smelling one of the blossoms. Presently, not looking at Vernon, 'I think,' she said, 'you had perhaps better beware of me.'

'For my sake or for yours?'

'Not for mine, certainly. There is little need for me to beware of anything.'

'Nor for me either,' said Vernon. 'You will not ruin my peace. I should perhaps be a better man if you were able to. Friendship is all I ask for. I neither expect more nor wish for it. As long as you care to meet me, let my heart throb as I think of you. If you withdraw your caring, no matter

how capriciously—well, I will not reproach
you.'

' I doubt,' she said smiling, 'if even I could
take things quite so easily as all that. However, we shall see—we shall see. We shall
have plenty of opportunities. And that
reminds me'—here all of a sudden her manner
became conventional—' I fear you called upon
us yesterday and did not find us at home. It is
my fault that you had your trouble for nothing.
I had written you a note myself the day
before, to say that we were called away, and
to ask you in my aunt's name to dine last
night with us. But—you see this is what it
is to be a methodical woman !—I left it on
my dressing-table, and it never was taken
at all. You would have only met Colonel
Stapleton.'

' What sort of man is Colonel Stapleton ?'
said Vernon abruptly. ' I barely know him to
speak to.'

'Oh,' she said carelessly, 'you can see what he is in a moment. He hunts and shoots, and has travelled over half the world. I am fond of him, for I've known him ever since I was *so* high; but there's nothing whatever in him; and I don't know that you missed much in not dining with us.'

'The night before,' said Vernon, 'I had a little dinner of my own. My guests were an old college friend, who, I am sorry to say, is gone; and a poor Catholic priest, who is staying near here for his health—an excellent man, but a little depressing sometimes.'

'A priest!' said Miss Walters.

'Not one of these country priests. My friend is an Englishman, whom I once knew well—a fellow called Frederic Stanley.—— You seem surprised. Do you know him? He is stopping here at the *Pension.*'

'Know him!' she replied. 'He is a sort

of cousin of mine, and is the truest friend I
ever had in the world. Mr. Vernon,' she
went on, 'whatever relationship yours and
mine may be, Frederic Stanley was *really*
like a brother to me. I could once have told
him anything ; I could have asked his advice
in anything. But I shall never do that again.
There is one thing gone from my life—gone
like many other things.'

' Why,' said Vernon, 'should his being a
priest estrange you ? '

' It doesn't,' she said. 'I was not thinking
of that. That, in itself, would rather help to
unite us. It is nothing that he knows of that
divides us now. Perhaps you—but let me
look once in your eyes again ; just look at me,
please, for one moment steadily—perhaps you
will know what it is some day. But about
Fred Stanley,' she went on. ' I should like
you very much to be friends with him ; I feel
so sure he could help you. I have an instinct,

in your case ; I have a power of divination which tells me so.'

'We are old friends already,' said Vernon ; 'we were at the same college together.'

'You are not yet friends in the way I wish you should be, or I am sure you would not have spoken of him as you did just this moment. You call him depressing, and I think I know what you mean by that. You remember him as he once was, full of feeling for art and poetry, and full of interest in everything from science to society ; and you misjudge the change in him.'

'In some men,' said Vernon, 'religion kindles poetry ; it seems to have quenched his. There is something now about him that is hard and prosaic.'

'If this is so, I can tell you the meaning of it. His right hand has offended him, and he has cut it off deliberately. There is no one who naturally is more alive to beauty, or

to whatever can flatter delicately ambition, intellectual pride, or the senses ; and under the
priest's surface, if you can only once get under
it, you will still discover the man of the world
and the poet ; only you will discover them
crucified. He has given his best as a sacrifice
to the God who, he thinks, loved men ; his
best, remember, not that which has cost him
nothing. You will detect his love for poetry
in his very silence about it. Try—to please
me, try—to make better friends with him.'

'I will try,' said Vernon, 'both for your
sake and for his. But tell me this, will you
—what you have just said makes me ask you
—are you yourself a Catholic ? '

' No,' she said with decision ; 'that is a
thing I never could be. I admire goodness,
and I hate evil—you might realise how
intensely, if you only knew my history ; and
amongst my Catholic friends have been the
best people I have known. But how, with

their eyes open, they can swallow so much nonsense—I suppose there is some explanation, but I confess it is quite beyond me.'

' What sort of nonsense ? '

' Frederic Stanley, for instance, thinks he could absolve me from my sins. I confess to him, and then he wipes the sin out. That is his notion. Now he might advise me, were I able to take advice, how to avoid repeating my sins ; but it is ridiculous even to fancy that he could relieve me of those I have committed.'

' It is quite as mysterious to me,' said Vernon, 'that God should forgive sins at all, as that He should forgive them through Stanley's agency.'

' It may be so,' she sighed. ' I don't know what to think about it. A God who is not merciful is a monster ; a God who is just and merciful seems an impossibility. Perhaps, after all, there is no mercy needed except from one human being to another ; and as to what we do to ourselves, perhaps that matters nothing.'

Vernon looked at her in surprise. ' Do you really think that ? ' he said.

She cast her eyes down, and began to put on her glove. She seemed occupied with the beauty of her own delicate hands. Presently however, and not without hesitation, ' I'll tell you,' she said, 'what I really do think. Religion, when a good man is possessed by it, makes him unselfish, and eager to work for others ; but it makes a woman selfish. It centres her whole anxiety on keeping her own robe taintless ; and it is always sending her to her looking-glass that she may examine her moral toilette. In the language of re-ligion, this is female virtue *par excellence.* Well, I can't help thinking—I hope you won't be shocked at me—that there are other virtues in God's eyes more important than this; and that it will be asked us first, what work have your hands done? not, whether we have kept them quite clean in doing it.'

'I have myself,' said Vernon slowly, and not without some surprise, 'been inclined to accuse Catholicism of the same fault in its teaching. But the fault—and I am sure it exists—is really not in Catholicism, but in certain times and teachers; perhaps, too, in certain pupils. What the Church teaches is, that we all of us, women as well as men, have two duties—one to ourselves, the other to humanity; and that these are like the two feet on which the pilgrim goes to God. It is easy to sneer at the self-regarding virtues; but the Church is a true philosopher when she insists to man on their necessity. Unless we work for others, we shall have nothing to offer God: unless we keep our hearts pure, we shall be unable to offer it.'

'Are you, then,' said Miss Walters, 'a Catholic?'

'I don't know,' he murmured, 'what I am.'

'Just now,' she said, 'you asked me a question, and I believe I evaded it. You asked me if I said my prayers. I am now going to ask the same question of you. Do you?'

'Very ill; but still I do say them.'

'Then if you do,' she said, holding out her hand to him, 'pray for me. Now, go. The clock is striking eight. I must get back to the house.'

Her hand was in his. He held it, and it was not withdrawn from him. Here again there was a sharp, distinct struggle in him. Should he do something, or should he forbear from doing it? Impulse urged him one way; conscience, with clear voice, the other: and in a few seconds again conscience yielded. Nearer and nearer to himself he drew his fair companion. She, as if spell-bound, offered no resistance. Presently he was sensible of the warmth of her face close to him: a moment more, and he had done what he said he longed to do ; he had kissed her on her sad, proud lips.

The touch recalled her to herself. 'Go,' she said, 'go! You don't know what it is you are doing to me.' And without another look she was gone.

Vernon found his way homewards in a new, confused excitement. A wild pleasure was struggling with self-reproach, and he hardly knew the exact nature of either. His mind was a mystery to himself, like a magician's crystal globe. There seemed to be in it a white vapour rising, which would take presently some unconjectured shape.

CHAPTER II.

THE after-taste of the above inter-view was to Vernon not without bitterness. He was beset by two reflections of an opposite nature, and each in its own way annoying. One of these was, 'I was a fool to kiss her.' The other, 'I was a still greater fool not to ask her when I might be allowed to see her again.' He had already made his formal call at the Château; he could not repeat it without some sort of invitation; and it might be a day, it might perhaps be even two, before his new romance could be proceeded with. Fate, however, proved more kind than he had anti-

cipated; for in the course of the morning
the following note arrived for him :

'Dear Mr. Vernon,' it ran, 'there is a
little town among the mountains here called
St. Paul du Var, which my aunt has seen from
a distance, and much wishes to visit. We
have some thoughts of going there this afternoon ; and if you have nothing better to do,
it would give her great pleasure if you would
come with us.

'Sincerely yours,

'CYNTHIA WALTERS.'

Then came the following postscript :

'Remember, if you are to be ever a
friend of mine, you must never act again as
if you were more than a friend.'

He seized a pen eagerly, and had begun
to write an acceptance, when he was cut short
by a very unwelcome interruption. The
mother had arrived of his little crippled *pro-*

légée, and was begging to speak to him about
her child's condition. ' Damn her ! ' was his
first exclamation ; and then to the servant he
said, ' Let her come to-morrow.' The man
closed the door, but in another moment
Vernon had recalled him. ' No,' he said ;
' you may tell her to come in now.' A breath
of garlic announced the old woman's advent.
Vernon forced a smile and held his handkerchief to his nostrils. The story was this :
the boot required altering ; one of the steel
supports grazed the poor child's ankle, and, so
far as Vernon could gather, she was in great
suffering. ' Let her take the boot off, and I
will come to-morrow.' It was on his lips to
say this, and to say it with some impatience.
But he happened to look into the old crone's
face, and his purpose altered. ' I will be
with you,' he said, ' in the course of the
next hour, and will take the child to Nice
with me, where the boot shall be refitted on

her.' Biting his lips with irritation, he wrote
Miss Walters an unwilling refusal, and started
presently on his distasteful work of mercy.
' I wish,' he murmured, ' the little animal was
at the devil. Here's another day she's spoilt
for me.' By-and-bye, however, he saw a
brighter side to the question. ' After all,' he
thought, ' it has perhaps turned out for the
best. Had I been with that girl, I should
have committed myself more and more. I
should have said much and meant nothing.
Or else—my God, what a brute I am!—I
should have been using the very thoughts
that I should like to hold most sacred as so
many dominoes in an idle game of love-
making. I have done that already this
morning. Campbell was right about me!'

Reflections such as these kept recurring to
him throughout the day; but they were not
without their rivals. The memory of Miss
Walters—her beauty, her delicate feeling, her

strange, ambiguous phrases, and the touch of her hand and lips—these would recur also, and make him again long for her company. His business with the child detained him some hours at Nice, and it was latish when he got home again. But the events of the day had done little to calm his mind. Prudence, desire, and conscience still stung and distracted him.

When he entered his library, he found another letter awaiting him, in an envelope not unlike the one he had received that morning. But he was disappointed; it was not from Miss Walters. It would have told its own authorship, even without the Duchess's signature. ' I hope,' it ran, ' that you have composed me those verses. However, it is not about these that I am writing; and I shall not dun you yet. What I want to tell you is that old Surbiton is coming over to the Cap to-morrow for me, to give a proper blowing up to the head gardener at the Hotel there ; and, as we all know how particular he is about his eating, I want you, if you will, to let him come to you for luncheon. If I may give you a hint, I will tell you he worships truffles. There's another man here—a good sort of creature in his way. You would perhaps, if he comes, let him trespass on your hospitality also.'

The prospect of any excitement pleased Vernon at the moment. He wrote out a telegram to the Duchess, that was to be sent the first thing next morning. He summoned his *chef,* and had a long conference with him about a luncheon: then, thoroughly wearied, he took himself off to bed ; and Lord Surbiton, truffles, and Miss Walters in turn engaged his thoughts, as by dreamy stages they decomposed into unconsciousness.

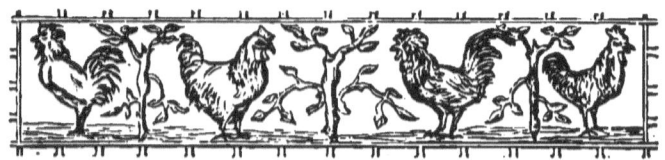

CHAPTER III.

E sent next day to the station to meet Lord Surbiton, who in due time arrived. He was not alone, however. The other man mentioned by the Duchess had escaped Vernon's mind for the moment; and it was with no great feeling of pleasure that he discovered it to be Colonel Stapleton. He had had a nodding acquaintance with the Colonel for many years previous; he had had a vague impression that he hunted, shot, and gambled; and he had had passing glimpses of him at various London houses. But as for thinking of

him for two minutes together, he had never done
this till the dinner at Monte Carlo. Colonel
Stapleton since that evening had been a vivid
personality to Vernon, and a personality distasteful to him to a degree he could not
account for. He was aware that in some
vague way he might regard the man as a
rival; but his distaste was different from the
mere distaste of jealousy. He grudged him
Miss Walters' acquaintance, not because there
was much that could attract her in him, but
because there was so little. ' Brute!' he had
murmured several times to himself, 'how I
hate those swimming eyes of his! I can't
bear to think that her eyes should look at
him.' This, however, he had himself seen
they had done; and whenever he recollected
how often and how smilingly, Miss Walters
seemed withdrawn from him to some mysterious estranging distance. But that was
not all. In the very process of this with-

drawal she became more alluring to him ; and he felt himself at such moments grow sick with a new longing for her.

The Colonel's reappearance made him again conscious of this ; and it required all his tact to prepare to receive him civilly. It was a moment's consolation to him, as he welcomed the two guests, to find that Lord Surbiton looked somewhat bored with his companion ; and Vernon at once, in his own mind, taxed the Duchess with the arrangement. Here at least he was right. Her Grace dearly loved arranging.

Matters, however, went better than he had hoped for. The Colonel's manner was one of extreme good breeding ; and his frank and evident shyness at intruding on a bare acquaintance, at once made Vernon genial without the trouble of trying to be so. Presently, too, at luncheon Lord Surbiton lit up into vivacity. All he had wanted hitherto had been some subject he could discuss strikingly ; and he soon found, in the science of good living, one suited equally to himself and his small audience.

'I often think,' said the Colonel, 'that the best meat I ever tasted was a piece of mutton in the desert, that was cooked for me by a young Coptic girl.'

Lord Surbiton turned to him with a keen glance in his eyes. 'The Coptic Church,' he said, 'shows a singular lenity, does it not, in its rule over the human affections ?'

'Certainly,' said the Colonel, 'when I studied its constitution, you could be married and unmarried by it, just as the fancy seized you. You could be married when you went to Egypt, and unmarried when you left it. What one gained by the arrangement was a wider field of choice.'

'But suppose,' said Lord Surbiton, 'one of these women became attached to you ;

might there not be some difficulty then in
getting quit of a lawful union ? '

' I shouldn't think so,' said the Colonel,
despatching a fine truffle. ' Besides, distance
can divorce one, as well as the Coptic Church.'

Lord Surbiton sighed. ' I regret much,'
he said, 'that I have hardly set foot in
Egypt; and I have yet been a constant
wanderer.   Like Shelley's *Alastor*,

.

> I have known
> Athens and Tyre, and Baalbec, and the waste
> Where stood Jerusalem.'

Colonel Stapleton stared. ' I, too, have
been in the East,' he said quietly. ' I was at
Jerusalem only a year ago.'

' Not,' said Vernon, ' as a religious pilgrim,
I suppose ? '

The Colonel brushed a speck of dirt from
his finely-shaped finger nail. ' No,' he said ;
' but I went there with a remarkably unre-
pentant Magdalene.   She had had something

to do with some one who had something to do
with India; and I came across her at a loose
end in Cairo. It was a curious thing to see
a woman of that kind amongst the sacred
scenes one has heard about, and all that kind
of thing. She, now—this woman—what
should you think her great wish was? Not
to see Olivet, or Jericho, or any of those
places. Upon my word I doubt if she had
ever even heard of Abraham. What she
wanted to see was a certain dance at
Damascus.'

Lord Surbiton's eyes shot with a fire of
intelligence, and his mouth emitted the ghost
of a hollow cackle. 'I know the dance you
mean,' he said. 'I've seen it myself several
times.'

'I mean this,' said the Colonel; and he
gave a minute description.

'I must confess,' said Vernon, 'that I
don't myself see the point of it.'

'Why, my dear fellow,' replied the Colonel in a slightly aggrieved tone, 'it's the most damned suggestive thing imaginable. Though, upon my word,' he went on, 'I don't know if it beats some of the plays in Paris. Have you, Lord Surbiton, seen—— ?' and he named a certain play and theatre. 'You have? Well, in the second act, did you ever notice how the women's dresses were cut?'

Lord Surbiton with regretful interest confessed that he had not. The Colonel at great length enlightened him. It was now Lord Surbiton's turn to impart instruction, and he repaid the Colonel in kind; it may also be said with usury. His vivid power both of imagination and description made most of what he said quite unfit to be chronicled; and the Colonel's eyes, as he listened, swam with attentive moisture.

By-and-by they all adjourned to the garden, where a table, under the myrtles, was set with wine and coffee. This turned Lord Surbiton's thoughts into quite a new direction, and, greatly to Vernon's pleasure, he began quoting Horace. Colonel Stapleton since he left Eton had been no great student; but the sound of the Latin tongue reminded him of one classical quotation. *Post prandia, Callirrhoe.* He had hardly aired this small fragment of learning, when his manner changed suddenly; and, slightly embarrassed, and not without some feeling of delicacy, 'That line,' he said, 'was not very well chosen by me, since, after Mr. Vernon's *prandium,* I have to call upon his next-door neighbours.'

'Confound him!' thought Vernon. 'What the devil does he come over here at all for?'

'But Colonel,' said Lord Surbiton, 'you are to help me as her Grace's emissary.'

'I will be back in half-an-hour, if our host will excuse me presently.'

An idea flashed upon Vernon. ' Will you
bring your friends with you,' he said, ' and
we will all see the Hotel garden together ? '

' Certainly,' said the Colonel, with gay
good humour. ' I forgot to ask you if you
had seen much of them, since that evening
when you carried them off in triumph. I
watched you as you drove away, and a fine,
spanking pace those horses of yours went,
too ? '

' Who are you talking of ? ' exclaimed
Lord Surbiton. ' Is it that lovely Miss
Walters ? By all means bring her, if such a
goddess will deign to appear among us.'

' Upon my word,' said the Colonel, ' she
is a nymph or a goddess. Did you ever
see any one with a turn of the neck like
that ? She's about the handsomest woman
in Europe — Miss Walters is ; at least,
that's my opinion ; and full of fun when you
only get to know her as I do. Then, the

dear old aunt too—what a capital old lady
that is! I've the greatest regard for Aunt
Louisa.'

'You, I suppose,' said Vernon, 'have
known them for a long time?'

'God bless my soul, yes! Why, when I
first knew Miss Cynthia she used to sit on
my knees and kiss me. But'—the Colonel
suddenly started, and his voice dropped with
alarm—'who's this coming here? It looks,
for all the world, like the parson.'

Vernon turned and saw it was Frederic
Stanley. 'Well,' said the Colonel hurriedly,
'I'm off to the Château, and in half-an-hour
I'll be back again.'

As for Stanley, he began with a quiet
apology: 'Your servant, Vernon, never told
me you had visitors; but merely said that I
should find you here in the garden.'

'Sit down, my dear fellow,' said Vernon;
'I'm perfectly charmed to see you.' But

he felt, at the same time, that the priest
was out of his element ; and was a little
nervous when he made him known to Lord
Surbiton.

The event, however, set all his fears to
rest. Lord Surbiton's versatility was more
than a fancied gift in him ; and on Stanley's
appearance his entire demeanour changed.
His furrowed face invested itself with a look
of thoughtful gravity ; and in his tone and
gesture, as he acknowledged his new acquaintance, there was the most perfect mixture of
fitting respect and dignity. Vernon thought,
as he watched him, that he had never seen
a truer gentleman. Stanley too, in becoming
a priest, had by no means forgotten the
savoir faire of the guardsman ; and now that
the Colonel was gone, the trio were presently
quite at ease together. The picturesqueness of
the scene was such as to strike all of them.
The blue of the sea that glowed through an

arch of myrtles, the glitter of the glasses, the red flash of the Burgundy, and the gold of the piled-up oranges, not to mention themselves in the green shadow—all this to three graceful scholars again suggested Horace, and the calm of the Horatian philosophy. Lord Surbiton broke out into several apt quotations, which both the others would in turn either cap or continue ; and he exclaimed presently with all his pomp of utterance, 'If every pleasure, as Epicurus said it did, springs somehow or other from some satisfaction of the senses, it is poetry, it is literature alone, that makes them last a lifetime.'

'Epicurus,' said Vernon, 'would, I think, have admitted that. He was the wisest, in his generation, of all the old philosophers ; and the popularity of Horace is one of the best proofs of this.'

'True,' said Lord Surbiton. 'There is

something, to me, much finer in the Epicurean
calm than in the Stoic fortitude. The man
who is stern, is repressing his emotion ; the
man who is calm has killed it. Think how
the two schools looked on death, for instance.
The Stoic looked on it with a defiant frown ;
by the act of an iron will he resolved not to
wince at it. He braved it—' and here in
Lord Surbiton's eyes came a slight flash of
the Devil—' as a clumsy but virtuous peasant
might brave some wicked nobleman. But
the Epicurean had no need of resolves, or for
making heroic faces. He met death, as
Metternich met Napoleon, with the reserved
grace of a man who is the superior in all but
power ; and who yet gives power its due.
Horace, as you say, Vernon, is a proof
of this. His odes show us more clearly
than anything the pathetic dignity, the
politely-concealed contempt, the easy self-
possession, and the superb high breeding,

with which the Epicurean poet greeted and treated death.'

' Whatever we think,' said Stanley, ' about the religious view of the matter, that sort of philosophy is now no longer possible.'

' Goethe's mother,' said Vernon, 'found it so ; and so did our Charles the Second.'

' I was thinking,' said Stanley, ' not of death then, but of life. What I meant was that a life of the proudest calm, though enriched with all the pleasures that can stimulate mind or body, is an ideal that now no man of insight can be satisfied with. We hear much, it is true, about the sublime calm of Goethe. I have almost thought myself that that sublime was very near the ridiculous. But, even were it not so, we are in Goethe's age no longer. There is a new spirit now abroad in the world ; we are becoming roused to the sense of a new duty. I am speaking of the modern conception of progress, and

the duty of each one of us to humanity.
Your Epicurean with his calm, in the face
of a thought like that, is like a man who
sits on his luggage when his train is leaving
the station.'

'Surely,' said Lord Surbiton, with a smile
of surprised courtesy, 'the Catholic Church
generally does not regard progress so com-
placently : and humanity as an object of
worship I should have conceived in her
eyes to be little better than Antichrist.'

'Do you remember the last words of an
expelled Pope on his death-bed, and the
answer his attendants made him—" Because
I have loved righteousness and hated iniquity,
therefore I die in exile " ? " Because God
has given thee the heathen for thine inherit-
ance, and the uttermost parts of the earth
for thy possession, Vicar of Christ, in exile
thou canst not die." Well, in the same way
one may speak of the Church always. She

cannot be outside progress, because she herself is everywhere. What she rejects in the
spirit of Modern Secularism, is not its truths,
but its false and delirious expression of them.
The religion of humanity, the religion of
human progress—these are really implicit parts
of her system ; and it is she alone that can give
them a reasoned meaning. Many people,
we know, think them to be new revelations.
Suppose we call them so. The life of the
Church is a series of new revelations. She is
human nature perpetually unfolding itself.'

'I should have conceived,' said Lord
Surbiton, 'that the Catholic type of sanctity
was a thing fixed for ever, and that it could
make no terms with progress.'

'That is true,' said Stanley, 'in one sense,
but it is not true in another : for change and
fixity are not of necessity incompatible. The
type of a perfect soldier may always remain
the same ; but it includes a change of conduct

according to changed conditions. His part
may be sometimes action ; sometimes a mute
vigilance : and it is the same with the saint,
in the world's changing ages. Myself I fully
recognise that we are now being swept
onwards into an era of new duties, and that
Almighty God may be demanding a larger
service from us.'

' I, too,' said Lord Surbiton, ' can tell that
a change is coming. You and Vernon will
see it ; but it will find the eyes of me and my
generation closed.' He was silent for a
minute or two, whilst he lighted a large cigar.
' I am not a Catholic, Mr. Stanley,' he resumed, ' but I am a student of human history ;
and, putting our obvious differences aside,
my view of the Church has been yours. I
am glad to find that I have so orthodox an
authority for it. She has seemed to me to
have embraced, and to have been the only
cause that has done so, all that the most

many-sided genius ever could or can be busy with. She was at once a perfect saint, and a perfect woman of the world, and she could understand all man's lowest impulses, and yet still for ever lead him up to the highest. Me,' he went on sighing, 'she has taught at least one lesson—that there is little in this world worth a regret on losing it.'

'You are the last person, my lord,' said Stanley with politeness, 'one could expect to hear say that. You have fame, position, fortune—all that the world can give you.'

'It is these blessings,' said Lord Surbiton, 'that have made my heart so teachable. It may be wisdom to despise the world; but to despise it thoroughly you must first possess it.'

These words were uttered with a ghastly kind of impressiveness, and received the reward they courted—a moment's complete silence. This was ended presently by sounds of a new quality. The music of female voices was suddenly heard approaching, and mixed with them came the Colonel's crackling laughter.

Vernon's heart had begun to beat quickly. He turned his head, and there was the group before him.

' You see,' said Lady Walters, ' we have come to return your visit ; and we hope you will show us your villa, as well as her Grace's gardens.' But Vernon had little time for thinking of Lady Walters. Her niece was there, standing side by side with the Colonel. She had just, as she said presently, been driving her pair of ponies ; and she still had on a tight-fitting cloth dress, beneath which protruded the tip of a varnished boot. The slightly masculine air which her present costume gave her, made a piquant mixture with her natural grace and softness. It seemed to hint to Vernon of some new side

to her character ; and it touched him, he
knew not why, with a quick twinge of jealousy.
The way she greeted him did not dispel this
feeling. She was perfectly frank and friendly :
she was, indeed, too frank. He sought in vain
from either her eye or hand any sign of their
strange, secret intimacy. 'Good heavens,
he thought, 'and it was but yesterday that I
kissed her!'

In an instant, however, he was distracted
by another scene enacting itself. Stanley,
hearing strangers approaching, had withdrawn
to a little distance. He had not even heard
that the Walters were at the Cap de Juan ;
and he now first learned the fact by finding
them there facing him. Vernon narrowly
watched Miss Walters, as the meeting was
taking place ; and he saw how truly she had
spoken when she called Stanley a brother. ' I
had been meaning,' she said. ' to have sent
you a note yesterday : but now to-night you

must come—won't you ?—and dine with us.'
Stanley assented, and directly afterwards
withdrew himself.

The next step with the others was now
to see Vernon's villa ; and Vernon in showing
it began to feel more prosperous. The
Colonel, it is true, showed a wish to engross
Miss Walters; but events at present would
often stand in his way. She was anxious to
be told about various books and pictures,
and on these points she could only appeal to
Vernon. Indeed for a good five minutes he
was almost *tête-à-tête* with her, as they turned
over together a portfolio of old engravings.
During this time their eyes met once ; and
for a moment hers softened as if in recogni-
tion of their intimacy. Directly afterwards,
however, came an odour of Ess bouquet, and,
looking up, Vernon saw the Colonel behind
them. ' Fine engravings,' said the latter,
' some of those, I should think.' And then

in an undertone, when Miss Walters' back
was turned, 'And devilish free, too, a lot of
those old plates are.' He said this with a
smile, and a glance at the closed portfolio.

Vernon answered him with extreme coldness. 'There is nothing, you may be sure,
that is free in that portfolio; or I should not
have been showing it to Miss Walters.' But
the Colonel was quite unwounded. He only
glanced over his shoulder to see that they
were unobserved, and pulled from his pocket
a small morocco book with a lock to it. 'If
you want,' he said, 'to see modern art, just
look into that. I got it at Nice this morning.'
Vernon looked, but it was for an instant only.
The contents were a series of photographs,
such as in England the police would seize
upon; and he gave it back with a curt 'Thank
you' to the Colonel.

The above incident, so far as Vernon's
peace was concerned, was the worst prepara-

tion possible for what was about to follow.
The party presently set out for the Hotel
gardens ; and, during the short walk thither,
kept more or less together. The head
gardener was summoned ; the directions of
the Duchess were given, and the little group
was on the point of moving on again. Vernon
looked towards Miss Walters, hoping she
might fall behind with him. A look was
enough ; he did not repeat it ; in an instant
he felt what had happened—she was attached
to Colonel Stapleton. Step by step did these
two separate themselves, letting the others
go on ahead of them, and pausing at times
on pretence of examining something, that
they might keep or increase their distance.
Vernon's heart was full of pain and bitterness,
and he walked almost silent by Lady Walters
and Lord Surbiton. Suddenly a surprise
was caused by the sight of another party,
which made his lordship exclaim, ' It's lucky

that her Grace isn't here !' The trespassers
proved to be a certain set from Nice, amongst
whom Vernon recognised a few of his own
acquaintance. Of this number was a certain
Mrs. Crane, one of the fairest and freest of
the married women of London. She not only
knew Vernon, but his companions also ; and,
quitting her own party, she advanced to meet
the others, whom a halt had again united.

'I'm dying,' said Mrs. Crane, 'to get out
on that reef of rocks there, but the people I'm
with have not got a spark of enterprise ; and
my boots have such high heels that I daren't
venture alone.'

'Let me be your guide,' said Vernon ; 'I
know the way perfectly.' And he fixed his
eyes on her with a look of shallow tenderness.

'I,' said Miss Walters, 'should like to come
too. I have often watched those rocks and
wished I could get out to them.'

The instant she spoke Vernon turned

sharp round to her. Mrs. Crane noticed the movement. But the impulses of the jealous reverse themselves in a flash of lightning, and the eager gesture was followed by the coldest of tones. ' The walk is perfectly easy,' he said, 'if Colonel Stapleton will give you a hand now and then. I have been there my-self continually.'

Both the elders declined so rough a pil-grimage, and the two younger couples set off by themselves, Miss Walters still with the Colonel, and Vernon with Mrs. Crane.

' Well, Mr. Vernon,' said that lady pre-sently, ' I've not seen you since that charming Sunday last summer, when we went down together on the drag to Maidenhead. At least I have seen you, though you were far too well occupied to take any notice of me. I saw you at Monte Carlo, and I saw, too, who it was you were talking to. However,' she added, as she glanced behind her towards

Miss Walters, 'you've a prettier one now to play with—that is, if Colonel Jack will allow you.'

'What has he got to do with it?' said Vernon, a little brusquely.

'What has not he? There he is now side by side with her. My good friend, don't you wish you were in the shoes of one of them?'

'Upon my word,' said Vernon, 'I can't say I do. If ever I want Miss Walters she is my next-door neighbour, so I could well spare her for an hour or two, even if all my heart were set on her. Besides, at the present moment, how could I even wish to better myself? You're very pretty, and I'm very agreeable ; and when there's nobody better to hand, you know quite well that you have a *caprice* for me.'

Love and its kindred feelings can make the wisest men like children, and when it does not make them children in the best sense

of the word, it will often make them childish in
the worst. It can not only bring back the
simplicity, but also the tempers, of the nursery.
Of these last, one of the least lovely forms is
a sullenness towards one person, expressed
by effusion towards another. It was this
form of temper which now overcame Vernon.
He could not spend his day in making love
to Miss Walters, so he resolved to spend it
in making love to Mrs. Crane. Nor was
Mrs. Crane in the least displeased at
this. It was strictly true that, amongst
a hundred other *caprices*, she had one
that she could quite distinguish for Vernon ;
and as all that she demanded of most
of her male friends was, not that their
devotion should be constant, but only that it
should recur on occasion, no jealousy of a
rival made her in the least cold or *difficile*.
Vernon and she were thus soon on the
tenderest terms, as they had often been before

for five or six hours together; and by the time they had reached the special rock they were making for, they were pretty well advanced in a very unmasked flirtation. This was just what Vernon in his present mood wished for; and when the two others joined them, and the four sat down together, he hoped that his conduct would not escape Miss Walters. This was a child's bit of temper, but he had a man's self-possession in showing it. He betrayed no sullenness to the person he wished to wound; he addressed her instead with an easy, genial indifference, which he knew would be more effective; and an intuitive sense thrilled him that each of his smiles was freezing her.

At first, however, when she looked about her she was lost in the lovely prospect. He could see how its beauty sank into her, like a stone into a clear well. 'What a contrast,' she said, 'between that grey cliff and the water ! And how one little plume of foam tosses over the sunken rock !'

'Yes, beautiful,' said Vernon civilly, with a slight, fatuous laugh. 'It's all as charming as can be ; though, for my own part, the love of scenery is one of the many things I have outlived, I think.'

Mrs. Crane patted him with her pretty gloved hand, and said, 'You tell that to your grandmother. Don't flatter yourself, my dear man, that you've outlived the sweets of life yet.'

'You are right,' said Vernon, as he looked at her ; 'for I have not outlived you.'

Mrs. Crane acknowledged the compliment with an impertinent little grimace, that became her admirably ; and then, turning sharp to the Colonel, she made an observation on a slight red mark on his temple. 'What on earth have you been up to ?' she said. 'Has Colonel Jack been fighting ?'

'Upon my soul,' cried the Colonel, 'it was something rather like it. What made the mark was a pistol bullet.' This announcement created the right surprise, but the Colonel plainly was talking with no eye to effect ; nor was there the least bravado in the way in which he told his story. He had been sleeping, it appeared, the preceding night at Nice ; and, arriving late there from Monte Carlo, he had walked to his hotel from the station. In a lonely place he had been beset by two men, it seemed with the intent of robbing him. 'One of the fellows,' he said, 'a little chap, I knocked down in a moment. The other fired a pistol at me ; and then, not seeing me fall, he bolted. There have been several cases of the same sort this winter ; and for the future,' he went on, producing a revolver, 'I shall not go out late without this.'

The weapon was a small one, finely

chased with silver, and Mrs. Crane inquired if it would really kill a man.

'It's killed two men already,' said the Colonel. 'If it hadn't been for that, I should have been a dead dog at Alexandria five years ago.'

The tone of the speaker was in all this so modest, that Vernon was conscious of a kind of grudging respect for him ; but what most amazed him was the aspect of Miss Walters. She was staring at the Colonel, not with the least interest or anxiety, but simply as if his face fascinated her. As for him, he was guiltless of any wish to be serious ; and his next observation showed it. 'Bless me, Miss Cynthia,' he said, putting his hand on her arm familiarly, 'what a knowing coat you've got on to-day ! Just turn my way and let me look at it. How many inches round in the waist does that make you ? '

She at once roused herself, and with a

smile and a frown together, 'Two inches more,' she said, 'than I should be without it.'

There was nothing in her manner that could be set down as coquetry ; yet Vernon, whose perceptions were in a super-sensitive state, detected something in it that made him turn sharp away from her. Presently they all rose, and began to set about returning.

Mrs. Crane, though she was not piqued on account of Miss Walters, was far too true a woman to be able to keep silent about her ; and as she and Vernon were descending the rocks together, she again opened the subject.

'Come,' she said, 'and tell me honestly how you like her.'

'I hardly know her,' said Vernon drily.

'Exactly ; and I doubt if you ever will. I've seen her at Florence before now ; and all the foreigners were at first sight in love with her. But it was at first sight only. She's as cold as ice afterwards. Every man I've heard speak of her, has told me the same story.'

'That fellow Stapleton,' said Vernon, 'seems to get on well enough with her.'

Mrs. Crane broke out into a little, malicious laugh. 'My dear man,' she said, 'I saw all along you were thinking so. I can see when a man's jealous as plainly as I can see what his necktie is. But you must be a goose if you're jealous of fat Jack Stapleton. He was a dangerous man once, I grant you ; but if he wants any conquests now, he has to go rather farther afield for them : and, from my own little observations at Monte Carlo, I suspect he goes farther afield pretty often. Besides, as for that girl there, he might just as well be her elder brother, or her uncle. He must have grown tired of kissing her before she was well out of the nursery. Just listen now, how she chatters to him. That's not the tone of a lover.'

Miss Walters' voice, it is true, was at that moment raised slightly. She was preparing to cross the last piece of broken ground ; and Vernon distinctly heard her, as she declined the Colonel's assistance. ' Thank you,' she said, ' I can get on quite well by myself. Really, my dear Jack, there's no need for you to be so affectionate.'

Vernon knew not why, but he uttered an inaudible oath to himself.

When they regained the gardens, Mrs. Crane found her own party had flown, and Lady Walters announced with a smile that Lord Surbiton had done so likewise. He had been carried off by a fascinating Polish countess. ' Why, it's the very woman,' said Mrs. Crane, ' that my own husband's in love with. And of course he's gone off too. Now, isn't that like a husband ? '

'My dear,' said Lady Walters, 'you needn't put yourself out. You know the train that they are going by, and I said that I would send you in our carriage to the station. Or if you like to wait for dinner, we should be very happy to see you. These gentlemen too, in case they have no other designs for themselves—we should be exceedingly glad if they would enliven us with their company.'

She looked round with an inquiry at Vernon and Colonel Stapleton. The latter at once assented; Vernon declined, having business, he said, that evening. 'Very well then,' smiled Lady Walters, 'we will hope for you at some other time.' He trusted that Miss Walters would take notice of this refusal; but he found she was standing even more near to him than he thought she was. The branch of a rose-tree had caught itself in her hat, and he heard her, in a constrained voice, asking him if he would disengage it for her. He was startled by her tone, and still more by the look she gave him. There was something in both of them, timid, piteous, and appealing. She reminded him of some wounded animal. He was in no mood, however, to be moved by impressions of this kind. He did the service she asked of him with the same easy politeness as heretofore; but when in the process, by accident, his hand touched her shoulder, he recoiled from it as if he had touched hot iron.

He discovered, the moment after, that Mrs. Crane as well as himself had declined Lady Walters' invitation; and a new inspiration seized him. 'Why should Lady Walters,' he said, 'be at the trouble of having her horses out? I can see Mrs. Crane to the station, if she has no objection to waiting here.'

Mrs. Crane's eyes flashed with a pleased intelligence ; and the matter was so settled.

'In that case,' said Miss Walters, 'we may as well be going back.' And the parties prepared to separate. As she took leave of Vernon, her voice seemed still unnatural, 'And are you *never*,' she murmured, 'coming to see me again ?' This was not, however, the last thing he heard of her ; for turning to her aunt she said, 'We may as well dine punctually, as Frederic Stanley does not like late hours.' These simple words had a sudden effect in one quarter. Colonel Stapleton with a frown drew Miss Walters apart a little ; his face changed ; he had evidently lost command of himself. 'What!' he exclaimed in an undertone, 'and is Mr. Stanley going to dine with you ?'

'He is,' she answered coldly. 'Do you happen to have any objection ?'

' Objection ! ' cried the Colonel, still between his teeth. ' My dear girl, are you an utter, absolute idiot ? What the Devil 's the good of my coming, if you've got that confounded parson with you ? '

END OF THE FIRST VOLUME.

LONDON : PRINTED BY
SPOTTISWOODE AND CO., NEW-STREET SQUARE
AND PARLIAMENT STREET

CHATTO & WINDUS'S
LIST OF BOOKS.

Crown 8vo, cloth extra, 3s. 6d. each.

The Wanderer's Library.

Merrie England in the Olden Time. By G. DANIEL. Illust.
Circus Life and Circus Celebrities. By THOMAS FROST.
Tavern Anecdotes and Sayings. By C. HINDLEY. Illustrated.
The Wilds of London. By JAMES GREENWOOD.
The Old Showmen and the Old London Fairs. By T. FROST.
The Story of the London Parks. By JACOB LARWOOD. Illust.
Low-Life Deeps. By JAMES GREENWOOD.
The Life and Adventures of a Cheap Jack. By C. HINDLEY.
The Lives of the Conjurors. By THOMAS FROST.
The World Behind the Scenes. By PERCY FITZGERALD.

NEW FINE-ART WORK. Large 4to, cloth extra, 21s.

Abdication, The:

An Historical Drama. By W. D. SCOTT-MONCRIEFF. With Seven
Original Etchings by JOHN PETTIE, R.A., W. Q. ORCHARDSON, R.A.,
J. MACWHIRTER, A.R.A., COLIN HUNTER, R. MACBETH, and TOM
GRAHAM. *[In preparation.*

Crown 8vo, Coloured Frontispiece and Illustrations, cloth gilt, 7s. 6d.

Advertising, A History of.

From the Earliest Times. Illustrated by Anecdotes, Curious Specimens, and Notes of Successful Advertisers. By HENRY SAMPSON.

Crown 8vo, cloth extra, with 639 Illustrations, 7s. 6d.

Architectural Styles, A Handbook of.

From the German of A. ROSENGARTEN by W. COLLETT-SANDARS.

Crown 8vo, with Portrait and Facsimile, cloth extra, 7s. 6d.

Artemus Ward's Works:

The Works of CHARLES FARRER BROWNE, better known as ARTEMUS
WARD. With Portrait, Facsimile of Handwriting, &c.

Bardsley (Rev. C. W.), Works by:

English Surnames : Their Sources and Significations. By
CHARLES WAREING BARDSLEY, M.A. Crown 8vo, cloth extra, 7s. 6d.

Curiosities of Puritan Nomenclature. By CHARLES W.
BARDSLEY. Crown 8vo, cloth extra, 7s. 6d.

Crown 8vo, cloth extra, 7s. 6d.

Bankers, A Handbook of London;

With some Account of their Predecessors, the Early Goldsmiths ; together with Lists of Bankers from 1677 to 1876. By F. G. HILTON PRICE.

A New Edition, crown 8vo, cloth extra, 7s. 6d.

Bartholomew Fair, Memoirs of.

By HENRY MORLEY. New Edition, with One Hundred Illustrations.

Imperial 4to, cloth extra, gilt and gilt edges, 21s. per volume.

Beautiful Pictures by British Artists :

A Gathering of Favourites from our Picture Galleries. In Two Series.

The FIRST SERIES including Examples by WILKIE, CONSTABLE,
TURNER, MULREADY, LANDSEER, MACLISE, E. M. WARD, FRITH,
Sir JOHN GILBERT, LESLIE, ANSDELL, MARCUS STONE, Sir NOEL
PATON, FAED, EYRE CROWE, GAVIN O'NEIL, and MADOX BROWN.

The SECOND SERIES containing Pictures by ARMITAGE, FAED,
GOODALL, HEMSLEY, HORSLEY, MARKS, NICHOLLS, Sir NOEL
PATON, PICKERSGILL, G. SMITH, MARCUS STONE, SOLOMON,
STRAIGHT, E. M. WARD, and WARREN.

All engraved on Steel in the highest style of Art. Edited, with
Notices of the Artists, by SYDNEY ARMYTAGE, M.A.

*" This book is well got up, and good engravings by Jeens, Lumb Stocks, and
others, bring back to us Royal Academy Exhibitions of past years."*—TIMES.

Small 4to, green and gold, 6s. 6d. ; gilt edges, 7s. 6d.

Bechstein's As Pretty as Seven,

And other German Stories. Collected by LUDWIG BECHSTEIN. With
Additional Tales by the Brothers GRIMM, and 100 Illustrations by
RICHTER.

NEW NOVEL BY THE AUTHOR OF " THE NEW REPUBLIC."

Belgravia for January, 1881,

Price One Shilling, contained the First Parts of Three New Serials,
viz. :—

1. A ROMANCE OF THE NINETEENTH CENTURY, by W. H. MALLOCK,
   Author of " The New Republic."
2. JOSEPH'S COAT, by D. CHRISTIE MURRAY, Author of "A Life's
   Atonement." With Illustrations by F. BARNARD.
3. ROUND ABOUT ETON AND HARROW, by ALFRED RIMMER. With
   numerous Illustrations.

*** The FORTY-THIRD Volume of BELGRAVIA, elegantly bound
in crimson cloth, full gilt side and back, gilt edges, price 7s. 6d., is now
ready.—Handsome Cases for binding volumes can be had at 2s. each.*

Demy 8vo, Illustrated, uniform in size for binding.

Blackburn's (Henry) Art Handbooks:

Academy Notes, 1875. With 40 Illustrations. 1s.
Academy Notes, 1876. With 107 Illustrations. 1s.
Academy Notes, 1877. With 143 Illustrations. 1s.
Academy Notes, 1878. With 150 Illustrations. 1s.
Academy Notes, 1879. With 146 Illustrations. 1s.
Academy Notes, 1880. With 126 Illustrations. 1s.
Grosvenor Notes, 1878. With 68 Illustrations. 1s.
Grosvenor Notes, 1879. With 60 Illustrations. 1s.
Grosvenor Notes, 1880. With 56 Illustrations. 1s.
Pictures at the Paris Exhibition, 1878. 80 Illustrations.
Pictures at South Kensington. (The Raphael Cartoons, Sheepshanks Collection, &c.) With 70 Illustrations. 1s.
The English Pictures at the National Gallery. With 114 Illustrations. 1s.
The Old Masters at the National Gallery. 128 Illusts. 1s. 6d.
Academy Notes, 1875-79. Complete in One Volume, with nearly 600 Illustrations in Facsimile. Demy 8vo, cloth limp, 6s.
A Complete Illustrated Catalogue to the National Gallery. With Notes by HENRY BLACKBURN, and 242 Illustrations. Demy 8vo cloth limp, 3s.

UNIFORM WITH "ACADEMY NOTES."

Royal Scottish Academy Notes, 1878. 117 Illustrations. 1s.
Royal Scottish Academy Notes, 1879. 125 Illustrations. 1s.
Royal Scottish Academy Notes, 1880. 114 Illustrations. 1s.
Glasgow Institute of Fine Arts Notes, 1878. 95 Illusts. 1s.
Glasgow Institute of Fine Arts Notes, 1879. 100 Illusts. 1s.
Glasgow Institute of Fine Arts Notes, 1880. 120 Illusts. 1s.
Walker Art Gallery Notes, Liverpool, 1878. 112 Illusts. 1s.
Walker Art Gallery Notes, Liverpool, 1879. 100 Illusts. 1s.
Walker Art Gallery Notes, Liverpool, 1880. 100 Illusts. 1s.
Royal Manchester Institution Notes, 1878. 88 Illustrations. 1s.
Society of Artists Notes, Birmingham, 1878. 95 Illusts. 1s.
Children of the Great City. By F. W. LAWSON. With Facsimile Sketches by the Artist. Demy 8vo, 1s.

Folio, half-bound boards, India Proofs, 21s.

Blake (William):

Etchings from his Works. By W. B. SCOTT. With descriptive Text.
" *The best side of Blake's work is given here, and makes a really attractive volume, which all can enjoy.* . . . *The etching is of the best kind, more refined and delicate than the original work.*"—SATURDAY REVIEW.

Crown 8vo, cloth extra, gilt, with Illustrations, 7s. 6d.

Boccaccio's Decameron;

or, Ten Days' Entertainment. Translated into English, with an Introduction by THOMAS WRIGHT, Esq., M.A., F.S.A. With Portrait, and STOTHARD'S beautiful Copperplates.

Bowers' (G.) Hunting Sketches:

Canters in Crampshire. By G. BOWERS. I. Gallops from Gorseborough. II. Scrambles with Scratch Packs. III. Studies with Stag Hounds. Oblong 4to, half-bound boards, 21s.

Leaves from a Hunting Journal. By G. BOWERS. Coloured in facsimile of the originals. Oblong 4to, half-bound, 21s.

Crown 8vo, cloth extra, gilt, 7s. 6d.

Brand's Observations on Popular Antiquities,

chiefly Illustrating the Origin of our Vulgar Customs, Ceremonies, and Superstitions. With the Additions of Sir HENRY ELLIS. An entirely New and Revised Edition, with fine full-page Illustrations.

Bret Harte, Works by:

Bret Harte's Collected Works. Arranged and Revised by the Author. Complete in Five Vols., crown 8vo, cloth extra, 6s. each.

Vol. I. COMPLETE POETICAL AND DRAMATIC WORKS. With Steel Plate Portrait, and an Introduction by the Author.

Vol. II. EARLIER PAPERS—LUCK OF ROARING CAMP, and other Sketches —BOHEMIAN PAPERS—SPANISH and AMERICAN LEGENDS.

Vol. III. TALES OF THE ARGONAUTS—EASTERN SKETCHES.

Vol. IV. GABRIEL CONROY.

Vol. V. STORIES—CONDENSED NOVELS, &c.

The Select Works of Bret Harte, in Prose and Poetry. With Introductory Essay by J. M. BELLEW, Portrait of the Author, and 50 Illustrations. Crown 8vo, cloth extra, 7s. 6d.

An Heiress of Red Dog, and other Stories. By BRET HARTE. Post 8vo, illustrated boards, 2s.; cloth limp, 2s. 6d.

The Twins of Table Mountain. By BRET HARTE. Fcap. 8vo, picture cover, 1s.; crown 8vo, cloth extra, 3s. 6d.

The Luck of Roaring Camp, and other Sketches. By BRET HARTE. Post 8vo, illustrated boards, 2s.

Jeff Briggs's Love Story. By BRET HARTE. Fcap. 8vo, picture cover, 1s.; cloth extra, 2s. 6d.

Small crown 8vo, cloth extra, gilt, with full-page Portraits, 4s. 6d.

Brewster's (Sir David) Martyrs of Science.

Small crown 8vo, cloth extra, gilt, with Astronomical Plates, 4s. 6d.

Brewster's (Sir D.) More Worlds than One,

the Creed of the Philosopher and the Hope of the Christian.

THE STOTHARD BUNYAN.—Crown 8vo, cloth extra, gilt, 7s. 6d.

Bunyan's Pilgrim's Progress.

Edited by Rev. T. SCOTT. With 17 beautiful Steel Plates by STOTHARD, engraved by GOODALL; and numerous Woodcuts.

Demy 8vo, cloth extra, 7s. 6d.

Burton's The Anatomy of Melancholy:

What it is; its Kinds, Causes, Symptoms, Prognostics, and several Cures of it. In Three Partitions; with their several Sections, Members, and Sub-sections, Philosophically, Medically, and Historically Opened and Cut-up. A New Edition, corrected and enriched by Translations of the Classical Extracts. *[In the press.*

Crown 8vo, cloth extra, gilt, with Illustrations, 7s. 6d.

Byron's Letters and Journals.
With Notices of his Life. By THOMAS MOORE. A Reprint of the Original Edition, newly revised, with Twelve full-page Plates.

Demy 8vo, cloth extra, 14s.

Campbell's (Sir G.) White and Black:
The Outcome of a Visit to the United States. By Sir GEORGE CAMPBELL, M.P.
" Few persons are likely to take it up without finishing it."—NONCONFORMIST.

Post 8vo, cloth extra, 1s. 6d.

Carlyle (Thomas) On the Choice of Books.
With Portrait and Memoir.

Crown 8vo, cloth extra, 7s. 6d.

Century (A) of Dishonour :
A Sketch of the United States Government's Dealings with some of the Indian Tribes.

Small 4to, cloth gilt, with Coloured Illustrations, 10s. 6d.

Chaucer for Children:
A Golden Key. By Mrs. H. R. HAWEIS. With Eight Coloured Pictures and numerous Woodcuts by the Author.

Demy 8vo, cloth limp, 2s. 6d.

Chaucer for Schools.
By Mrs. HAWEIS, Author of "Chaucer for Children."
" We hail with pleasure the appearance of Mrs. Haweis's 'Chaucer for Schools.' Her account of 'Chaucer the Tale-teller' is certainly the pleasantest, chattiest, and at the same time one of the soundest descriptions of the old master, his life and works and general surroundings, that have ever been written. The chapter cannot be too highly praised."—ACADEMY.

Crown 8vo, cloth extra, gilt, 7s. 6d.

Colman's Humorous Works :
"Broad Grins," "My Nightgown and Slippers," and other Humorous Works, Prose and Poetical, of GEORGE COLMAN. With Life by G. B. BUCKSTONE, and Frontispiece by HOGARTH.

Conway (Moncure D.), Works by:
Demonology and Devil-Lore. By MONCURE D. CONWAY, M.A. Two Vols., royal 8vo, with 65 Illustrations, 28s.
" A valuable contribution to mythological literature. . . . There is much good writing, a vast fund of humanity, undeniable earnestness, and a delicate sense of humour, all set forth in pure English."—CONTEMPORARY REVIEW.
A Necklace of Stories. By MONCURE D. CONWAY, M.A. Illustrated by W. J. HENNESSY. Square 8vo, cloth extra, 6s.
" This delightful ' Necklace of Stories' is inspired with lovely and lofty sentiments."—ILLUSTRATED LONDON NEWS.
The Wandering Jew, and the Pound of Flesh. By MONCURE D. CONWAY, M.A. Crown 8vo, cloth extra, 4s. 6d. *[In the e..*

Crown 8vo, cloth limp, with Map and Illustrations, 2*s.* 6*d.*

Cleopatra's Needle:

Its Acquisition and Removal to England. By Sir J. E. ALEXANDER.

Demy 8vo, cloth extra, with Coloured Illustrations and Maps, 24*s.*

Cope's History of the Rifle Brigade

(The Prince Consort's Own), formerly the 95th. By Sir WILLIAM
H. COPE, formerly Lieutenant, Rifle Brigade.

Crown 8vo, cloth extra, 7*s.* 6*d.*

Cornwall.—Popular Romances of the West

of England ; or, The Drolls, Traditions, and Superstitions of Old
Cornwall. Collected and Edited by ROBERT HUNT, F.R.S. New
and Revised Edition, with Additions, and Two Steel-plate Illustrations
by GEORGE CRUIKSHANK.

Crown 8vo, cloth extra, gilt, with 13 Portraits, 7*s.* 6*d.*

Creasy's Memoirs of Eminent Etonians ;

with Notices of the Early History of Eton College. By Sir EDWARD
CREASY, Author of "The Fifteen Decisive Battles of the World."

Crown 8vo, cloth extra, with Etched Frontispiece, 7*s.* 6*d.*

Credulities, Past and Present.

By WILLIAM JONES, F.S.A., Author of "Finger-Ring Lore," &c.

Two Vols., demy 4to, handsomely bound in half-morocco, gilt, profusely
Illustrated with Coloured and Plain Plates and Woodcuts, price £7 7*s.*

Cyclopædia of Costume ;

or, A Dictionary of Dress—Regal, Ecclesiastical, Civil, and Military—
from the Earliest Period in England to the reign of George the Third.'
Including Notices of Contemporaneous Fashions on the Continent,
and a General History of the Costumes of the Principal Countries of
Europe. By J. R. PLANCHÉ, Somerset Herald.

·The Volumes may also be had *separately* (each Complete in itself) at £3 13*s.*6*d.* each **:**

Vol. I. THE DICTIONARY.
Vol. II. A GENERAL HISTORY OF COSTUME IN EUROPE.

Also in 25 Parts, at 5*s.* each. Cases for binding, 5*s.* each.

"*A comprehensive and highly valuable book of reference. . . . We have
rarely failed to find in this book an account of an article of dress, while in most
of the entries curious and instructive details are given. . . . Mr. Planché's
enormous labour of love, the production of a text which, whether in its dictionary
form or in that of the 'General History,' is within its intended scope immeasurably
the best and richest work on Costume in English. . . . This book is not only
one of the most readable works of the kind, but intrinsically attractive and
amusing.*"—ATHENÆUM.

"*A most readable and interesting work—and it can scarcely be consulted in
vain, whether the reader is in search for information as to military, court,
ecclesiastical, legal, or professional costume. . . . All the chromo-lithographs,
and most of the woodcut illustrations— the latter amounting to several thousands
—are very elaborately executed ; and the work forms a* livre de luxe *which renders
it equally suited to the library and the ladies' drawing-room.*"—TIMES.

NEW WORK by the AUTHOR OF "PRIMITIVE MANNERS AND CUSTOMS."—Crown 8vo, cloth extra, 6s.

Crimes and Punishments.

Including a New Translation of Beccaria's "Dei Delitti e delle Pene."
By JAMES ANSON FARRER.

Crown 8vo, cloth gilt, Two very thick Volumes, 7s. 6d. each.

Cruikshank's Comic Almanack.

Complete in TWO SERIES: The FIRST from 1835 to 1843; the SECOND from 1844 to 1853. A Gathering of the BEST HUMOUR of THACKERAY, HOOD, MAYHEW, ALBERT SMITH, A'BECKETT, ROBERT BROUGH, &c. With 2,000 Woodcuts and Steel Engravings by CRUIKSHANK, HINE, LANDELLS, &c.

Square 8vo, cloth gilt, profusely Illustrated, 10s. 6d.

Dickens.—About England with Dickens.

With Illustrations by ALFRED RIMMER and CHARLES A. VANDER-HOOF.   *[In preparation.*

Second Edition, revised and enlarged, demy 8vo, cloth extra,
with Illustrations, 24s.

Dodge's (Colonel) The Hunting Grounds of

the Great West: A Description of the Plains, Game, and Indians of the Great North American Desert. By RICHARD IRVING DODGE, Lieutenant-Colonel of the United States Army. With an Introduction by WILLIAM BLACKMORE; Map, and numerous Illustrations drawn by ERNEST GRISET.

Demy 8vo, cloth extra, 12s. 6d.

Doran's Memories of our Great Towns.

With Anecdotic Gleanings concerning their Worthies and their Oddities. By Dr. JOHN DORAN, F.S.A.

Two Vols., crown 8vo, cloth extra, 21s.

Drury Lane (Old):

Fifty Years' Recollections of Author, Actor, and Manager. By EDWARD STIRLING.

"Mr. Stirling's two volumes of theatrical recollections contain, apart from the interest of his own early experiences, when the London stage was a very different thing from what it now is, a quantity of amusing and interesting facts and anecdotes, new and old. The book is one which may be taken up in a spare quarter of an hour or half-hour with a tolerable certainty of lighting upon something of interest."—SATURDAY REVIEW.

Demy 8vo, cloth, 16s.

Dutt's India, Past and Present;

with Minor Essays on Cognate Subjects. By SHOSHEE CHUNDER DUTT, Rái Bábádoor.

Crown 8vo, cloth boards, 6s. per Volume.

Early English Poets.

Edited, with Introductions and Annotations, by Rev. A. B. GROSART.

"Mr. Grosart has spent the most laborious and the most enthusiastic care on the perfect restoration and preservation of the text. . . From Mr. Grosart we always expect and always receive the final results of most patient and competent scholarship."—EXAMINER.

1. **Fletcher's (Giles, B.D.) Complete Poems**: Christ's Victorie in Heaven, Christ's Victorie on Earth, Christ's Triumph over Death, and Minor Poems. With Memorial-Introduction and Notes. One Vol.

2. **Davies' (Sir John) Complete Poetical Works**, including Psalms I. to L. in Verse, and other hitherto Unpublished MSS., for the first time Collected and Edited. Memorial-Introduction and Notes. Two Vols.

3. **Herrick's (Robert) Hesperides, Noble Numbers, and Complete Collected Poems.** With Memorial-Introduction and Notes, Steel Portrait, Index of First Lines, and Glossarial Index, &c. Three Vols.

4. **Sidney's (Sir Philip) Complete Poetical Works**, including all those in "Arcadia." With Portrait, Memorial-Introduction, Essay on the Poetry of Sidney, and Notes. Three Vols.

Imperial 8vo, with 147 fine Engravings, half-morocco, 36s.

Early Teutonic, Italian, and French Masters

(The). Translated and Edited from the Dohme Series, by A. H. KEANE, M.A.I. With numerous Illustrations.

"Cannot fail to be of the utmost use to students of art history."—TIMES.

Crown 8vo, cloth extra, gilt, with Illustrations, 6s.

Emanuel On Diamonds and Precious

Stones; their History, Value, and Properties; with Simple Tests for ascertaining their Reality. By HARRY EMANUEL, F.R.G.S. With numerous Illustrations, Tinted and Plain.

Demy 4to, cloth extra, with Illustrations, 36s.

Emanuel and Grego.—A History of the Gold-

smith's and Jeweller's Art in all Ages and in all Countries. By E. EMANUEL and JOSEPH GREGO. With numerous fine Engravings.

[In preparation.

Crown 8vo, cloth extra, with Illustrations, 7s. 6d.

Englishman's House, The:

A Practical Guide to all interested in Selecting or Building a House, with full Estimates of Cost, Quantities, &c. By C. J. RICHARDSON. Third Edition. With nearly 600 Illustrations.

Crown 8vo, cloth extra, 6s.

Evolutionist (The) At Large.

By GRANT ALLEN.

"Mr. Allen's method of treatment, as explanatory of the scientific revolution known as evolution, gives a sort of personality and human character to the trout or the strawberry blossom, which invests them with additional charm, and makes many of his pages read more like a fanciful fairy tale than a scientific work. . . . . Mr. Allen's essays ought to open many a half-closed eye."—MANCHESTER EXAMINER.

Crown 8vo, cloth extra, with nearly 300 Illustrations, 7s. 6d.

Evolution (Chapters on);

A Popular History of the Darwinian and Allied Theories of Development. By ANDREW WILSON, Ph.D., F.R.S. Edin. &c. [*In preparation.*

Abstract of Contents :—The Problem Stated—Sketch of the Rise and Progress of Evolution—What Evolution is and what it is not—The Evidence for Evolution—Evidence from Development—Evidence from Rudimentary Organs—Evidence from Geographical Distribution—Evidence from Geology—Evolution and Environments—Flowers and their Fertilisation and Development—Evolution and Degeneration—Evolution and Ethics—The Relations of Evolution to Ethics and Theology, &c. &c.

Two Vols., crown 8vo, cloth extra, 21s.

Ewald.—Stories from the State Papers.

By ALEX. CHARLES EWALD. [*In preparation.*

Folio, cloth extra, £1 11s. 6d.

Examples of Contemporary Art.

Etchings from Representative Works by living English and Foreign Artists. Edited, with Critical Notes, by J. COMYNS CARR.

" *It would not be easy to meet with a more sumptuous, and at the same time a more tasteful and instructive drawing-room book.*"—NONCONFORMIST.

Crown 8vo, cloth extra, with Illustrations, 6s.

Fairholt's Tobacco :

Its History and Associations ; with an Account of the Plant and its Manufacture, and its Modes of Use in all Ages and Countries. By F. W. FAIRHOLT, F.S.A. With Coloured Frontispiece and upwards of 100 Illustrations by the Author.

Crown 8vo, cloth extra, with Illustrations, 4s. 6d.

Faraday's Chemical History of a Candle.

Lectures delivered to a Juvenile Audience. A New Edition. Edited by W. CROOKES, F.C.S. With numerous Illustrations.

Crown 8vo, cloth extra, with Illustrations, 4s. 6d.

Faraday's Various Forces of Nature.

New Edition. Edited by W. CROOKES, F.C.S. Numerous Illustrations.

Crown 8vo, cloth extra, with Illustrations, 7s. 6d.

Finger-Ring Lore :

Historical, Legendary, and Anecdotal. By WM. JONES, F.S.A. With Hundreds of Illustrations of Curious Rings of all Ages and Countries.

" *One of those gossiping books which are as full of amusement as of instruction.*"—ATHENÆUM.

NEW NOVEL BY JUSTIN McCARTHY.

Gentleman's Magazine for January, 1881,

Price One Shilling, contained the First Chapters of a New Novel, entitled "THE COMET OF A SEASON," by JUSTIN MCCARTHY, M.P., Author of "A History of Our Own Times," "Dear Lady Disdain," &c. SCIENCE NOTES, by W. MATTIEU WILLIAMS, F.R.A.S., will also be continued Monthly.

*** *Now ready, the Volume for* JULY *to* DECEMBER, *1880, cloth extra, price* 8s. 6d.*; and Cases for binding, price* 2s. *each.*

THE RUSKIN GRIMM.—Square 8vo, cloth extra, 6s. 6d. ;
gilt edges, 7s. 6d.

German Popular Stories.

Collected by the Brothers GRIMM, and Translated by EDGAR TAYLOR.
Edited with an Introduction by JOHN RUSKIN. With 22 Illustrations
after the inimitable designs of GEORGE CRUIKSHANK. Both Series
Complete.

*" The illustrations of this volume . . . are of quite sterling and admirable
art, of a class precisely parallel in elevation to the character of the tales which
they illustrate; and the original etchings, as I have before said in the Appendix to
my ' Elements of Drawing,' were unrivalled in masterfulness of touch since Rem-
brandt (in some qualities of delineation, unrivalled even by him). . . . To make
somewhat enlarged copies of them, looking at them through a magnifying glass,
and never putting two lines where Cruikshank has put only one, would be an exer-
cise in decision and severe drawing which would leave afterwards little to be learnt
in schools."—Extract from Introduction by* JOHN RUSKIN.

Post 8vo, cloth limp, 2s. 6d.

Glenny's A Year's Work in Garden and

Greenhouse : Practical Advice to Amateur Gardeners as to the Management of the Flower, Fruit, and Frame Garden. By GEORGE GLENNY.
*" A great deal of valuable information, conveyed in very simple language. The
amateur need not wish for a better guide."*—LEEDS MERCURY.

Crown 8vo, cloth gilt and gilt edges, 7s. 6d.

Golden Treasury of Thought, The:

An ENCYCLOPÆDIA OF QUOTATIONS from Writers of all Times and
Countries. Selected and Edited by THEODORE TAYLOR.

New and Cheaper Edition, demy 8vo, cloth extra, with Illustrations, 7s.6d.

Greeks and Romans, The Life of the,

Described from Antique Monuments. By ERNST GUHL and W.
KONER. Translated from the Third German Edition, and Edited by
Dr. F. HUEFFER. With 545 Illustrations.

Crown 8vo, cloth extra, gilt, with Illustrations, 7s. 6d.

Greenwood's Low-Life Deeps:

An Account of the Strange Fish to be found there. By JAMES GREEN-
WOOD. With Illustrations in tint by ALFRED CONCANEN.

Crown 8vo, cloth extra, gilt, with Illustrations, 7s. 6d.

Greenwood's Wilds of London:

Descriptive Sketches, from Personal Observations and Experience, of
Remarkable Scenes, People, and Places in London. By JAMES GREEN-
WOOD. With 12 Tinted Illustrations by ALFRED CONCANEN.

Crown 8vo, cloth extra, gilt, with Illustrations, 4s. 6d.

Guyot's Earth and Man;

or, Physical Geography in its Relation to the History of Mankind.
With Additions by Professors AGASSIZ, PIERCE, and GRAY ; 12 Maps
and Engravings on Steel, some Coloured, and copious Index.

Square 16mo (Tauchnitz size), cloth extra, 2s. per volume.

Golden Library, The:

Ballad History of England. By W. C. BENNETT.

Bayard Taylor's Diversions of the Echo Club.

Byron's Don Juan.

Emerson's Letters and Social Aims.

Godwin's (William) Lives of the Necromancers.

Holmes's Autocrat of the Breakfast Table. With an Introduction by G. A. SALA.

Holmes's Professor at the Breakfast Table.

Hood's Whims and Oddities. Complete. With all the original Illustrations.

Irving's (Washington) Tales of a Traveller.

Irving's (Washington) Tales of the Alhambra.

Jesse's (Edward) Scenes and Occupations of Country Life.

Lamb's Essays of Elia. Both Series Complete in One Vol.

Leigh Hunt's Essays: A Tale for a Chimney Corner, and other Pieces. With Portrait, and Introduction by EDMUND OLLIER.

Mallory's (Sir Thomas) Mort d'Arthur: The Stories of King Arthur and of the Knights of the Round Table. Edited by B. MONTGOMERIE RANKING.

Pascal's Provincial Letters. A New Translation, with Historical Introduction and Notes, by T. M'CRIE, D.D.

Pope's Poetical Works. Complete.

Rochefoucauld's Maxims and Moral Reflections. With Notes, and an Introductory Essay by SAINTE-BEUVE.

St. Pierre's Paul and Virginia, and The Indian Cottage. Edited, with Life, by the Rev. E. CLARKE.

Shelley's Early Poems, and Queen Mab, with Essay by LEIGH HUNT.

Shelley's Later Poems: Laon and Cythna, &c.

Shelley's Posthumous Poems, the Shelley Papers, &c.

Shelley's Prose Works, including A Refutation of Deism, Zastrozzi, St. Irvyne, &c.

White's Natural History of Selborne. Edited, with additions, by THOMAS BROWN, F.L.S.

Hake (Dr. Thomas Gordon), Poems by:

Maiden Ecstasy. Small 4to, cloth extra, 8s.

New Symbols. Crown 8vo, cloth extra, 6s.

Legends of the Morrow. Crown 8vo, cloth extra, 6s.

Medium 8vo, cloth extra, gilt, with Illustrations, 7s. 6d.

Hall's (Mrs. S. C.) Sketches of Irish Character.

With numerous Illustrations on Steel and Wood by MACLISE, GILBERT, HARVEY, and G. CRUIKSHANK.

*"The Irish Sketches of this lady resemble Miss Mitford's beautiful English sketches in ' Our Village,' but they are far more vigorous and picturesque and bright."—*BLACKWOOD'S MAGAZINE.

Post 8vo, cloth extra, 4s. 6d.; a few large-paper copies, half-Roxb., 10s. 6d.

Handwriting, The Philosophy of.

By Don FELIX DE SALAMANCA. With 134 Facsimiles of Signatures.

Haweis (Mrs.), Works by:

The Art of Dress. By Mrs. H. R. HAWEIS. Illustrated by the Author. Small 8vo, illustrated cover, 1s.; cloth limp, 1s. 6d.

"*A well-considered attempt to apply canons of good taste to the costumes of ladies of our time. . . . . Mrs. Haweis writes frankly and to the point, she does not mince matters, but boldly remonstrates with her own sex on the follies they indulge in. . . . . We may recommend the book to the ladies whom it concerns.*"—ATHENÆUM.

The Art of Beauty. By Mrs. H. R. HAWEIS. Square 8vo, cloth extra, gilt, gilt edges, with Coloured Frontispiece and nearly 100 Illustrations, 10s. 6d.

The Art of Decoration. By Mrs. H. R. HAWEIS. Small 4to, handsomely bound and profusely Illustrated, 10s. 6d.   [*In the press.*

** *See also* CHAUCER, *p. 5 of this Catalogue.*

SPECIMENS OF MODERN POETS.—Crown 8vo, cloth extra, 6s.

Heptalogia (The); or, The Seven against Sense.

A Cap with Seven Bells.

" *Of really good parodies it would be difficult to name more than half-a-dozen outside the 'Anti-Jacobin,' the 'Rejected Addresses,' and the 'Ballads of Bon Gaultier.' . . . It is no slight praise to say that the volume before us bears comparison with these celebrated collections. . . . But the merits of the book cannot be fairly estimated by means of a few extracts; it should be read at length to be appreciated properly, and, in our opinion, its merits entitle it to be very widely read indeed.*"—ST. JAMES'S GAZETTE.

Cr. 8vo, bound in parchment, 8s.; Large-Paper copies (only 50 printed), 15s.

Herbert.—The Poems of Lord Herbert of

Cherbury. Edited, with an Introduction, by J. CHURTON COLLINS.
[*In the press.*

History of Hertfordshire.

By JOHN EDWIN CUSSANS.

This Magnificent Work, ranging with the highest class of County Histories, the result of many years' labour, is now completed, and in course of delivery to Subscribers.

It is comprised in Eight Parts, imperial quarto, each containing the complete History of one of the Eight Hundreds into which the County is divided, with separate Pagination, Title, and Index. Each Part contains about 350 pages, and is printed in the most careful manner on fine paper, with full-page Plates on Steel and Stone, and a profusion of smaller Engravings on Wood of objects of interest in the County, and the Arms of the principal Landowners, together with elaborate Pedigrees (126 in all), now for the first time printed.

The price to Subscribers is Two Guineas each complete Part. Purchasers are guaranteed the possession of a work of constantly increasing value by the fact that only three hundred and fifty copies are printed, the greater number of which are already subscribed for.

Seventy-five copies only, numbered and signed by the Author, have been specially printed on Large Paper (Royal Folio), price Four Guineas each Part.

Complete in Four Vols., demy 8vo, cloth extra, 12s. each.

History of Our Own Times, from the Accession
of Queen Victoria to the General Election of 1880. By JUSTIN
MCCARTHY, M.P.

*"Criticism is disarmed before a composition which provokes little but approval.
This is a really good book on a really interesting subject, and words piled on words
could say no more for it."* — SATURDAY REVIEW.

Crown 8vo, cloth extra, 5s.

Hobhouse's The Dead Hand :
Addresses on the subject of Endowments and Settlements of Property.
By Sir ARTHUR HOBHOUSE, Q.C., K.C.S.I.

Crown 8vo, cloth extra, 4s. 6d.

Hollingshead's (John) Plain English.
*"I anticipate immense entertainment from the perusal of Mr. Hollingshead's
'Plain English,' which I imagined to be a philological work, but which I find to
be a series of essays, in the Hollingsheadian or Sledge-Hammer style, on those
matters theatrical with which he is so eminently conversant."* — G. A. S. in the
ILLUSTRATED LONDON NEWS.

Crown 8vo, cloth limp, with Illustrations, 2s. 6d.

Holmes's The Science of Voice Production
and Voice Preservation : A Popular Manual for the Use of Speakers
and Singers. By GORDON HOLMES, L.R.C.P.E.

Crown 8vo, cloth extra, gilt, 7s. 6d.

Hood's (Thomas) Choice Works,
In Prose and Verse. Including the CREAM OF THE COMIC ANNUALS.
With Life of the Author, Portrait, and Two Hundred Illustrations.

Square crown 8vo, cloth extra, gilt edges, 6s.

Hood's (Tom) From Nowhere to the North
Pole : A Noah's Arkæological Narrative. With 25 Illustrations by
W. BRUNTON and E. C. BARNES.

*"The amusing letterpress is profusely interspersed with the jingling rhymes
which children love and learn so easily. Messrs. Brunton and Barnes do full
justice to the writer's meaning, and a pleasanter result of the harmonious co-
operation of author and artist could not be desired."* — TIMES.

Crown 8vo, cloth extra, gilt, 7s. 6d.

Hook's (Theodore) Choice Humorous Works,
including his Ludicrous Adventures, Bons-mots, Puns, and Hoaxes.
With a new Life of the Author, Portraits, Facsimiles, and Illustrations.

Crown 8vo, cloth extra, 7s.

Horne's Orion :
An Epic Poem in Three Books. By RICHARD HENGIST HORNE.
With a brief Commentary by the Author. With Photographic Portrait
from a Medallion by SUMMERS. Tenth Edition.

Crown 8vo, cloth extra, 7s. 6d.

Howell's Conflicts of Capital and Labour

Historically and Economically considered. Being a History and Review of the Trade Jnions of Great Britain, showing their Origin, Progress, Constitution, and Objects, in their Political, Social, Economical, and Industriol Aspects. By GEORGE HOWELL.

"This book is an attemp , and on the whole a successful attempt, to place the work of trade unions in the 'ast. and their objects in the future, fairly before the public from the working man s point of view."—PALL MALL GAZETTE.

Demy 8vo, cloth extra, 12s. 6d.

Hueffer's The Troubadours:

A History of Provencal Life and Literature in the Middle Ages. By FRANCIS HUEFFER.

Crown 8vo, cloth extra, 6s.

Janvier.—Practical Keramics for Students.

By C. A. JANVIER.

"Will be found a useful handbook by those who wish to try the manufacture or decoration of pottery, and may be studied by all who desire to know something of the art."—MORNING POST.

A NEW EDITION, Revised and partly Re-written, with several New Chapters and Illustrations, crown 8vo, cloth extra, 7s. 6d.

Jennings' The Rosicrucians:

Their Rites and Mysteries. With Chapters on the Ancient Fire and Serpent Worshippers. By HARGRAVE JENNINGS. With Five full-page Plates and upwards of 300 Illustrations.

Jerrold (Tom), Works by:

Our Kitchen Garden : The Plants we Grow, and How we Cook Them. By TOM JERROLD, Author of "The Garden that Paid the Rent," &c. Post 8vo, cloth limp, 2s. 6d.

"The combination of hints on cookery with gardening has been very cleverly carried out, and the result is an interesting and highly instructive little work. Mr. Jerrold is correct in saying that English people do not make half the use of vegetables they might ; and by showing how easily they can be grown, and so obtained fresh, he is doing a great deal to make them more popular."—DAILY CHRONICLE.

Household Horticulture : A Gossip about Flowers. By TOM JERROLD. Post 8vo, cloth limp, 2s. 6d. *[In the press.*

Two Vols. 8vo, with 52 Illustrations and Maps, cloth extra, gilt, 14s.

Josephus, The Complete Works of.

Translated by WHISTON. Containing both "The Antiquities of the Jews" and "The Wars of the Jews."

Small 8vo, cloth, full gilt, gilt edges, with Illustrations, 6s.

Kavanaghs' Pearl Fountain,

And other Fairy Stories. By BRIDGET and JULIA KAVANAGH. With Thirty Illustrations by J. MOYR SMITH.

"Genuine new fairy stories of the old type, some of them as delightful as the best of Grimm's ' German Popular Stories.' . . . . For the most part the stories are downright, thorough-going fairy stories of the most admirable kind. . . Mr. Moyr Smith's illustrations, too, are admirable."—SPECTATOR.

Crown 8vo, illustrated boards, with numerous Plates, 2s. 6d.

Lace (Old Point), and How to Copy and

Imitate it. By DAISY WATERHOUSE HAWKINS. With 17 Illustrations by the Author.

Crown 8vo, cloth extra, gilt, with Portraits, 7s. 6d.

Lamb's Complete Works,

In Prose and Verse, reprinted from the Original Editions, with many Pieces hitherto unpublished. Edited, with Notes and Introduction, by R. H. SHEPHERD. With Two Portraits and Facsimile of a Page of the "Essay on Roast Pig."

"*A complete edition of Lamb's writings, in prose and verse, has long been wanted, and is now supplied. The editor appears to have taken great pains to bring together Lamb's scattered contributions, and his collection contains a number of pieces which are now reproduced for the first time since their original appearance in various old periodicals.*"—SATURDAY REVIEW.

Crown 8vo, cloth extra, with numerous Illustrations, 10s. 6d.

Lamb (Mary and Charles):

Their Poems, Letters, and Remains. With Reminiscences and Notes by W. CAREW HAZLITT. With HANCOCK's Portrait of the Essayist, Facsimiles of the Title-pages of the rare First Editions of Lamb's and Coeridge's Works, and numerous Illustrations.

"*Very many passages will delight those fond of literary trifles; hardly any portion will fail in interest for lovers of Charles Lamb and his sister.*"—STANDARD.

Small 8vo, cloth extra, 5s.

Lamb's Poetry for Children, and Prince

Dorus. Carefully Reprinted from unique copies.

"*The quaint and delightful little book, over the recovery of which all the hearts of his lovers are yet warm with rejoicing.*"—A. C. SWINBURNE.

Demy 8vo, cloth extra, with Maps and Illustrations, 18s.

Lamont's Yachting in the Arctic Seas;

or, Notes of Five Voyages of Sport and Discovery in the Neighbourhood of Spitzbergen and Novaya Zemlya. By JAMES LAMONT, F.R.G.S. With numerous full-page Illustrations by Dr. LIVESAY.

"*After wading through numberless volumes of icy fiction, concocted narrative, and spurious biography of Arctic voyagers, it is pleasant to meet with a real and genuine volume. . . . He shows much tact in recounting his adventures, and they are so interspersed with anecdotes and information as to make them anything but wearisome. . . . The book, as a whole, is the most important addition made to our Arctic literature for a long time.*"—ATHENÆUM.

Crown 8vo, cloth, full gilt, 7s. 6d.

Latter-Day Lyrics:

Poems of Sentiment and Reflection by Living Writers; selected and arranged, with Notes, by W. DAVENPORT ADAMS. With a Note on some Foreign Forms of Verse, by AUSTIN DOBSON.

Crown 8vo, cloth extra, 6s.

Lares and Penates;

Or, The Background of Life.   By FLORENCE CADDY.

" *The whole book is well worth reading, for it is full of practical suggestions.
. . . . We hope nobody will be deterred from taking up a book which teaches a
good deal about sweetening poor lives as well as giving grace to wealthy ones."—*
GRAPHIC.

Crown 8vo, cloth, full gilt, 6s.

Leigh's A Town Garland.

By HENRY S. LEIGH, Author of "Carols of Cockayne."

" *If Mr. Leigh's verse survive to a future generation—and there is no reason
why that honour should not be accorded productions so delicate, so finished, and so
full of humour—their author will probably be remembered as the Poet of the
Strand."—*ATHENÆUM.

SECOND EDITION.—Crown 8vo, cloth extra, with Illustrations, 6s.

Leisure-Time Studies, chiefly Biological.

By ANDREW WILSON, F.R.S.E., Lecturer on Zoology and Compara-
tive Anatomy in the Edinburgh Medical School.

"*It is well when we can take up the work of a really qualified investigator,
who in the intervals of his more serious professional labours sets himself to impart
knowledge in such a simple and elementary form as may attract and instruct,
with no danger of misleading the tyro in natural science. Such a work is this
little volume, made up of essays and addresses written and delivered by Dr.
Andrew Wilson, lecturer and examiner in science at Edinburgh and Glasgow, at
leisure intervals in a busy professional life. . . . Dr. Wilson's pages teem with
matter stimulating to a healthy love of science and a reverence for the truths
of nature."—*SATURDAY REVIEW.

Crown 8vo, cloth extra, with Illustrations, 7s. 6d.

Life in London;

or, The History of Jerry Hawthorn and Corinthian Tom. With the
whole of CRUIKSHANK'S Illustrations, in Colours, after the Originals.

Crown 8vo, cloth extra, 6s.

Lights on the Way:

Some Tales within a Tale.   By the late J. H. ALEXANDER, B.A.
Edited, with an Explanatory Note, by H. A. PAGE, Author of
"Thoreau: A Study."

Crown 8vo, cloth extra, with Illustrations, 7s. 6d.

Longfellow's Complete Prose Works.

Including "Outre Mer," "Hyperion," "Kavanagh," "The Poets
and Poetry of Europe," and "Driftwood." With Portrait and Illustrations by VALENTINE BROMLEY.

Crown 8vo, cloth extra, gilt, with Illustrations, 7s. 6d.

Longfellow's Poetical Works.

Carefully Reprinted from the Original Editions. With numerous
fine Illustrations on Steel and Wood.

Crown 8vo, cloth extra, 5s.

Lunatic Asylum, My Experiences in a.

By a SANE PATIENT.

" *The story is clever and interesting, sad beyond measure though the subject be. There is no personal bitterness, and no violence or anger. Whatever may have been the evidence for our author's madness when he was consigned to an asylum, nothing can be clearer than his sanity when he wrote this book; it is bright, calm, and to the point.*"—SPECTATOR.

Demy 8vo, with Fourteen full-page Plates, cloth boards, 18s.

Lusiad (The) of Camoens.

Translated into English Spenserian verse by ROBERT FFRENCH DUFF, Knight Commander of the Portuguese Royal Order of Christ.

Macquoid (Mrs.), Works by:

In the Ardennes. By KATHARINE S. MACQUOID. With 50 fine Illustrations by THOMAS R. MACQUOID. Uniform with " Pictures and Legends." Square 8vo, cloth extra, 10s. 6d.

" *This is another of Mrs. Macquoid's pleasant books of travel, full of useful information, of picturesque descriptions of scenery, and of quaint traditions respecting the various monuments and ruins which she encounters in her tour. . . . To such of our readers as are already thinking about the year's holiday, we strongly recommend the perusal of Mrs. Macquoid's experiences. The book is well illustrated by Mr. Thomas R. Macquoid.*"—GRAPHIC.

Pictures and Legends from Normandy and Brittany. By KATHARINE S. MACQUOID. With numerous Illustrations by THOMAS R. MACQUOID. Square 8vo, cloth gilt, 10s. 6d.

" *Mr. and Mrs. Macquoid have been strolling in Normandy and Brittany, and the result of their observations and researches in that picturesque land of romantic associations is an attractive volume, which is neither a work of travel nor a collection of stories, but a book partaking almost in equal degree of each of these characters. . . . The illustrations, which are numerous, are drawn, as a rule, with remarkable delicacy as well as with true artistic feeling.*"—DAILY NEWS.

Through Normandy. By KATHARINE S. MACQUOID. With 90 Illustrations by T. R. MACQUOID. Square 8vo, cloth extra, 7s. 6d.

" *One of the few books which can be read as a piece of literature, whilst at the same time handy in the knapsack.*"—BRITISH QUARTERLY REVIEW.

Through Brittany. By KATHARINE S. MACQUOID. With numerous Illustrations by T. R. MACQUOID. Sq. 8vo, cloth extra, 7s. 6d.

" *The pleasant companionship which Mrs. Macquoid offers, while wandering from one point of interest to another, seems to throw a renewed charm around each oft-depicted scene.*"—MORNING POST.

Crown 8vo, cloth extra, with Illustrations, 2s. 6d.

Madre Natura v. The Moloch of Fashion.

By LUKE LIMNER. With 32 Illustrations by the Author. FOURTH EDITION, revised and enlarged.

Handsomely printed in facsimile, price 5s.

Magna Charta.

An exact Facsimile of the Original Document in the British Museum, printed on fine plate paper, nearly 3 feet long by 2 feet wide, with the Arms and Seals emblazoned in Gold and Colours.

Mallock's (W. H.) Works:

Is Life Worth Living? By WILLIAM HURRELL MALLOCK.
New Edition, crown 8vo, cloth extra, 6s.

"*This deeply interesting volume. . . . . It is the most powerful vindication of religion, both natural and revealed, that has appeared since Bishop Butler wrote, and is much more useful than either the Analogy or the Sermons of that great divine, as a refutation of the peculiar form assumed by the infidelity of the present day. . . . . Deeply philosophical as the book is, there is not a heavy page in it. The writer is 'possessed,' so to speak, with his great subject, has sounded its depths, surveyed it in all its extent, and brought to bear on it all the resources of a vivid, rich, and impassioned style, as well as an adequate acquaintance with the science, the philosophy, and the literature of the day.*"—IRISH DAILY NEWS.

The New Republic; or, Culture, Faith, and Philosophy in an English Country House. By W. H. MALLOCK. Post 8vo, cloth limp, 2s. 6d.

The New Paul and Virginia; or, Positivism on an Island. By W. H. MALLOCK. Post 8vo, cloth limp, 2s. 6d.

Poems. By W. H. MALLOCK. Small 4to, bound in parchment, 8s.

A Romance of the Nineteenth Century. By W. H. MALLOCK. Two Vols., crown 8vo.   [*In the press.*

Mark Twain's Works:

The Choice Works of Mark Twain. Revised and Corrected throughout by the Author. With Life, Portrait, and numerous Illustrations. Crown 8vo, cloth extra, 7s. 6d.

The Adventures of Tom Sawyer. By MARK TWAIN. With 100 Illustrations. Small 8vo, cloth extra, 7s. 6d. CHEAP EDITION, illustrated boards, 2s.

A Pleasure Trip on the Continent of Europe : The Innocents Abroad, and The New Pilgrim's Progress. By MARK TWAIN. Post 8vo, illustrated boards, 2s.

An Idle Excursion, and other Sketches. By MARK TWAIN. Post 8vo, illustrated boards, 2s.

A Tramp Abroad. By MARK TWAIN. With 314 Illustrations. Crown 8vo, cloth extra, 7s. 6d.

"*The fun and tenderness of the conception, of which no living man but Mark Twain is capable, its grace and fantasy and slyness, the wonderful feeling for animals that is manifest in every line, make of all this episode of Jim Baker and his jays a piece of work that is not only delightful as mere reading, but also of a high degree of merit as literature. . . . The book is full of good things, and contains passages and episodes that are equal to the funniest of those that have gone before.*"—ATHENÆUM.

Milton (J. L.), Works by:

The Hygiene of the Skin. A Concise Set of Rules for the Management of the Skin; with Directions for Diet, Wines, Soaps, Baths, &c. By J. L. MILTON, Senior Surgeon to St. John's Hospital. Small 8vo, 1s.; cloth extra, 1s. 6d.

The Bath in Diseases of the Skin. Small 8vo, 1s.; cloth extra, 1s. 6d.

Post 8vo, cloth limp, 2*s*. 6*d*. per vol.

Mayfair Library, The:

The New Republic. By W. H. MALLOCK.

The New Paul and Virginia. By W. H. MALLOCK.

The True History of Joshua Davidson. By E. LYNN LINTON.

Old Stories Re-told. By WALTER THORNBURY.

Thoreau : His Life and Aims. By H. A. PAGE.

By Stream and Sea. By WILLIAM SENIOR.

Jeux d'Esprit. Edited by HENRY S. LEIGH.

Puniana. By the Hon. HUGH ROWLEY.

More Puniana. By the Hon. HUGH ROWLEY.

Puck on Pegasus. By H. CHOLMONDELEY-PENNELL.

The Speeches of Charles Dickens. With Chapters on Dickens as Letter-Writer and Public Reader.

Muses of Mayfair. Edited by H. CHOLMONDELEY-PENNELL.

Gastronomy as a Fine Art. By BRILLAT-SAVARIN.

The Philosophy of Hand-writing. By DON FELIX DE SALAMANCA.

Latter-Day Lyrics. Edited by W. DAVENPORT ADAMS.

Original Plays by W. S. GILBERT. FIRST SERIES.

Original Plays by W. S. GILBERT. SECOND SERIES.

Carols of Cockayne. By HENRY S. LEIGH.

Literary Frivolities, Fancies, Follies, and Frolics. By WILLIAM T. DOBSON.

Pencil and Palette : Biographical Anecdotes chiefly of Contemporary Painters, with Gossip about Pictures Lost, Stolen, and Forged, also Great Picture Sales. By ROBERT KEMPT.

The Book of Clerical Anecdotes : A Gathering of the Antiquities, Humours, and Eccentricities of "The Cloth." By JACOB LARWOOD.

The Agony Column of |"The Times," from 1800 to 1870. Edited, with an Introduction, by ALICE CLAY.

The Cupboard Papers. By FIN-BEC.

Quips and Quiddities. Selected by W. DAVENPORT ADAMS. [*In press.*

Pastimes and Players. By ROBERT MACGREGOR. [*In the press.*

Melancholy Anatomised : A Popular Abridgment of "Burton's Anatomy of Melancholy." [*In press.*

** Other Volumes are in preparation.

New Novels.

THE BLACK ROBE. By WILKIE COLLINS. Three Vols. crown 8vo.

THE CHAPLAIN OF THE FLEET. By WALTER BESANT and JAMES RICE. Three Vols., crown 8vo.

FROM EXILE. By JAMES PAYN, Author of "By Proxy," "A Confidential Agent," &c. Three Vols., crown 8vo.

A ROMANCE OF THE NINETEENTH CENTURY. By W. H. MALLOCK. Two Vols., crown 8vo. [*In the press.*

MY LOVE. By E. LYNN LINTON. Three Vols. [*In the press.*

A VILLAGE COMMUNE. By OUIDA. Two Vols.

TEN YEARS' TENANT. By BESANT and RICE. Three Vols.

A CONFIDENTIAL AGENT. By JAMES PAYN. Three Vols.

A LIFE'S ATONEMENT. By D. C. MURRAY. Three Vols.

QUEEN COPHETUA. By R. E. FRANCILLON. Three Vols.

THE LEADEN CASKET. By Mrs. HUNT. Three Vols.

REBEL OF THE FAMILY. By E. L. LINTON. Three Vols.

Small 8vo, cloth limp, with Illustrations, 2*s.* 6*d.*

Miller's Physiology for the Young;

Or, The House of Life: Human Physiology, with its Applications to the Preservation of Health. For use in Classes and Popular Reading. With numerous Illustrations. By Mrs. F. FENWICK MILLER.

" An admirable introduction to a subject which all who value health and enjoy life should have at their fingers' ends."—ECHO.

Square 8vo, cloth extra, with numerous Illustrations, 7*s.* 6*d.*

North Italian Folk.

By Mrs. COMYNS CARR. Illustrated by RANDOLPH CALDECOTT.

" A delightful book, of a kind which is far too rare. If anyone wants to really know the North Italian folk, we can honestly advise him to omit the journey, and read Mrs. Carr's pages instead. . . Description with Mrs. Carr is a real gift. . It is rarely that a book is so happily illustrated."—CONTEMPORARY REVIEW.

Crown 8vo, cloth extra, with Vignette Portraits, price 6*s.* per Vol.

Old Dramatists, The:

Ben Jonson's Works.
With Notes, Critical and Explanatory, and a Biographical Memoir by WILLIAM GIFFORD. Edited by Colonel CUNNINGHAM. Three Vols.

Chapman's Works.
Now First Collected. Complete in Three Vols. Vol. I. contains the Plays complete, including the doubtful ones; Vol. II. the Poems and Minor Translations, with an Introductory Essay

by ALGERNON CHARLES SWINBURNE.
Vol. III. the Translations of the Iliad and Odyssey.

Marlowe's Works.
Including his Translations. Edited, with Notes and Introduction, by Col. CUNNINGHAM. One Vol.

Massinger's Plays.
From the Text of WILLIAM GIFFORD. With the addition of the Tragedy of " Believe as you List." Edited by Col. CUNNINGHAM. One Vol.

Crown 8vo, red cloth extra, 5*s.* each.

Ouida's Novels.—Library Edition.

Held in Bondage.	By OUIDA.	**Dog of Flanders.**	By OUIDA.
Strathmore.	By OUIDA.	**Pascarel.**	By OUIDA.
Chandos.	By OUIDA.	**Two Wooden Shoes.**	By OUIDA.
Under Two Flags.	By OUIDA.	**Signa.**	By OUIDA.
Idalia.	By OUIDA.	**In a Winter City.**	By OUIDA.
Cecil Castlemaine.	By OUIDA.	**Ariadne.**	By OUIDA.
Tricotrin.	By OUIDA.	**Friendship.**	By OUIDA.
Puck.	By OUIDA.	**Moths.**	By OUIDA.
Folle Farine.	By OUIDA.	**Pipistrello.**	By OUIDA.

. Also a Cheap Edition of all but the last two, post 8vo, illustrated boards, 2*s.* each.

Post 8vo, cloth limp, 1*s.* 6*d.*

Parliamentary Procedure, A Popular Handbook of. By HENRY W. LUCY.

Crown 8vo, cloth extra, with Portrait and Illustrations, 7*s.* 6*d.*

Poe's Choice Prose and Poetical Works.

With BAUDELAIRE'S " Essay."

LIBRARY EDITIONS, mostly Illustrated, crown 8vo, cloth extra, 3*s*. 6*d*. each.

Piccadilly Novels, The.

Popular Stories by the Best Authors.

Maid, Wife, or Widow? By Mrs. ALEXANDER.

Ready-Money Mortiboy. By W. BESANT and JAMES RICE.

My Little Girl. By W. BESANT and JAMES RICE.

The Case of Mr. Lucraft. By W. BESANT and JAMES RICE.

This Son of Vulcan. By W. BESANT and JAMES RICE.

With Harp and Crown. By W. BESANT and JAMES RICE.

The Golden Butterfly. By W. BESANT and JAMES RICE.

By Celia's Arbour. By W. BESANT and JAMES RICE.

The Monks of Thelema. By W. BESANT and JAMES RICE.

'Twas in Trafalgar's Bay. By W. BESANT and JAMES RICE.

The Seamy Side. By WALTER BESANT and JAMES RICE.

Antonina. By WILKIE COLLINS.

Basil. By WILKIE COLLINS.

Hide and Seek. W. COLLINS.

The Dead Secret. W. COLLINS.

Queen of Hearts. W. COLLINS.

My Miscellanies. W. COLLINS.

The Woman in White. By WILKIE COLLINS.

The Moonstone. W. COLLINS.

Man and Wife. W. COLLINS.

Poor Miss Finch. W. COLLINS.

Miss or Mrs.? By W. COLLINS.

The New Magdalen. By WILKIE COLLINS.

The Frozen Deep. W. COLLINS.

The Law and the Lady. By WILKIE COLLINS.

The Two Destinies. By WILKIE COLLINS.

The Haunted Hotel. By WILKIE COLLINS.

The Fallen Leaves. By WILKIE COLLINS.

Jezebel's Daughter. W. COLLINS.

Deceivers Ever. By Mrs. H. LOVETT CAMERON.

Juliet's Guardian. By Mrs. H. LOVETT CAMERON.

Felicia. M. BETHAM-EDWARDS.

Olympia. By R. E. FRANCILLON.

The Capel Girls. By EDWARD GARRETT.

Robin Gray. CHARLES GIBBON.

For Lack of Gold. By CHARLES GIBBON.

In Love and War. By CHARLES GIBBON.

What will the World Say? By CHARLES GIBBON.

For the King. CHARLES GIBBON.

In Honour Bound. By CHARLES GIBBON.

Queen of the Meadow. By CHARLES GIBBON.

In Pastures Green. By CHARLES GIBBON.

Under the Greenwood Tree. By THOMAS HARDY.

Garth. By JULIAN HAWTHORNE.

Ellice Quentin. By JULIAN HAWTHORNE.

Thornicroft's Model. By Mrs. A. W. HUNT.

Fated to be Free. By JEAN INGELOW.

Confidence. HENRY JAMES, Jun.

The Queen of Connaught. By HARRIETT JAY.

The Dark Colleen. By H. JAY.

Number Seventeen. By HENRY KINGSLEY.

Oakshott Castle. H. KINGSLEY.

Patricia Kemball. By E. LYNN LINTON.

PICCADILLY NOVELS—*continued.*

The Atonement of Leam Dundas. By E. LYNN LINTON.

The World Well Lost. By E. LYNN LINTON.

Under which Lord? By E. LYNN LINTON.

With a Silken Thread. By E. LYNN LINTON.

The Waterdale Neighbours. By JUSTIN MCCARTHY.

My Enemy's Daughter. By JUSTIN MCCARTHY.

Linley Rochford. By JUSTIN MCCARTHY.

A Fair Saxon. By JUSTIN MCCARTHY.

Dear Lady Disdain. By JUSTIN MCCARTHY.

Miss Misanthrope. By JUSTIN MCCARTHY.

Donna Quixote. By JUSTIN MCCARTHY.

Quaker Cousins. By AGNES MACDONELL.

Lost Rose. By KATHARINE S. MACQUOID.

The Evil Eye. By KATHARINE S. MACQUOID.

Open! Sesame! By FLORENCE MARRYAT.

Written in Fire. F. MARRYAT.

Touch and Go. By JEAN MIDDLEMASS.

Whiteladies. Mrs. OLIPHANT.

The Best of Husbands. By JAMES PAYN.

Fallen Fortunes. JAMES PAYN.

Halves. By JAMES PAYN.

Walter's Word. JAMES PAYN.

What He Cost Her. J. PAYN.

Less Black than we're Painted. By JAMES PAYN.

By Proxy. By JAMES PAYN.

Under One Roof. JAMES PAYN.

High Spirits. By JAMES PAYN.

Her Mother's Darling. By Mrs. J. H. RIDDELL.

Bound to the Wheel. By JOHN SAUNDERS.

Guy Waterman. J. SAUNDERS.

One Against the World. By JOHN SAUNDERS.

The Lion in the Path. By JOHN SAUNDERS.

The Way We Live Now. By ANTHONY TROLLOPE.

The American Senator. By ANTHONY TROLLOPE.

Diamond Cut Diamond. By T. A. TROLLOPE.

Post 8vo, illustrated boards, 2s. each.

Popular Novels, Cheap Editions of.

[WILKIE COLLINS' NOVELS and BESANT and RICE'S NOVELS may also be had in cloth limp at 2s. 6d. *See, too, the* PICCADILLY NOVELS, *for Library Editions.*]

Maid, Wife, or Widow? By Mrs. ALEXANDER.

Ready-Money Mortiboy. By WALTER BESANT and JAMES RICE.

With Harp and Crown. By WALTER BESANT and JAMES RICE.

This Son of Vulcan. By W. BESANT and JAMES RICE.

My Little Girl. By the same.

The Case of Mr. Lucraft. By WALTER BESANT and JAMES RICE.

The Golden Butterfly. By W. BESANT and JAMES RICE.

By Celia's Arbour. By WALTER BESANT and JAMES RICE.

The Monks of Thelema. By WALTER BESANT and JAMES RICE.

'Twas in Trafalgar's Bay. By WALTER BESANT and JAMES RICE.

Seamy Side. BESANT and RICE.

Grantley Grange. By S. BEAUCHAMP.

POPULAR NOVELS—*continued.*

An Heiress of Red Dog. By BRET HARTE.

The Luck of Roaring Camp. By BRET HARTE.

Gabriel Conroy. BRET HARTE.

Surly Tim. By F. E. BURNETT.

Juliet's Guardian. By Mrs. H. LOVETT CAMERON.

Deceivers Ever. By Mrs. L. CAMERON.

Cure of Souls. By MACLAREN COBBAN.

Antonina. By WILKIE COLLINS.

Basil. By WILKIE COLLINS.

Hide and Seek. W. COLLINS.

The Dead Secret. W. COLLINS.

The Queen of Hearts. By WILKIE COLLINS.

My Miscellanies. W. COLLINS.

The Woman in White. By WILKIE COLLINS.

The Moonstone. W. COLLINS.

Man and Wife. W. COLLINS.

Poor Miss Finch. W. COLLINS.

Miss or Mrs. ? W. COLLINS.

New Magdalen. By W. COLLINS.

The Frozen Deep. W. COLLINS.

The Law and the Lady. By WILKIE COLLINS.

The Two Destinies. By WILKIE COLLINS.

The Haunted Hotel. By WILKIE COLLINS.

Fallen Leaves. By W. COLLINS.

Felicia. M. BETHAM-EDWARDS.

Roxy. By EDWARD EGGLESTON.

Filthy Lucre. By ALBANY DE FONBLANQUE.

Olympia. By R. E. FRANCILLON.

The Capel Girls. By EDWARD GARRETT.

Robin Gray. By CHAS. GIBBON.

For Lack of Gold. By CHARLES GIBBON.

What will the World Say ? By CHARLES GIBBON.

In Honour Bound. By CHAS. GIBBON.

In Love and War. By CHARLES GIBBON.

For the King. By CHARLES GIBBON.

Queen of the Meadow. By CHARLES GIBBON.

Dick Temple. By JAMES GREENWOOD.

Every-day Papers. By A. HALLIDAY.

Under the Greenwood Tree. By THOMAS HARDY.

Garth. By JULIAN HAWTHORNE.

Thornicroft's Model. By Mrs. A. HUNT.

Fated to be Free. By JEAN INGELOW.

Confidence. By HENRY JAMES, Jun.

The Queen of Connaught. By HARRIETT JAY.

The Dark Colleen. By H. JAY.

Number Seventeen. By HENRY KINGSLEY.

Oakshott Castle. H. KINGSLEY.

Patricia Kemball. By E. LYNN LINTON.

The Atonement of Leam Dundas By E. LYNN LINTON.

The World Well Lost. By E. LYNN LINTON.

Under which Lord ? By Mrs. LINTON.

The Waterdale Neighbours. By JUSTIN McCARTHY.

Dear Lady Disdain. By the same.

My Enemy's Daughter. By JUSTIN McCARTHY.

A Fair Saxon. J. McCARTHY.

Linley Rochford. McCARTHY.

Miss Misanthrope. McCARTHY.

Donna Quixote. J. McCARTHY.

POPULAR NOVELS—*continued.*

The Evil Eye. By KATHARINE S. MACQUOID.

Lost Rose. K. S. MACQUOID.

Open! Sesame! By FLORENCE MARRYAT.

Wild Oats. By F. MARRYAT.

Little Stepson. F. MARRYAT.

Fighting the Air. F. MARRYAT.

Touch and Go. By JEAN MIDDLEMASS.

Mr. Dorillion. J. MIDDLEMASS.

Whiteladies. By Mrs. OLIPHANT.

Held in Bondage. By OUIDA.

Strathmore. By OUIDA.

Chandos. By OUIDA.

Under Two Flags. By OUIDA.

Idalia. By OUIDA.

Cecil Castlemaine. By OUIDA.

Tricotrin. By OUIDA.

Puck. By OUIDA.

Folle Farine. By OUIDA.

Dog of Flanders. By OUIDA.

Pascarel. By OUIDA.

Two Little Wooden Shoes. By OUIDA.

Signa. By OUIDA.

In a Winter City. By OUIDA.

Ariadne. By OUIDA.

Friendship. By OUIDA.

Walter's Word. By J. PAYN.

Best of Husbands. By J. PAYN.

Halves. By JAMES PAYN.

Fallen Fortunes. By J. PAYN.

What He Cost Her. J. PAYN.

Less Black than We're Painted. By JAMES PAYN.

By Proxy. By JAMES PAYN.

Under One Roof. By J. PAYN.

High Spirits. By JAS. PAYN.

The Mystery of Marie Roget. By EDGAR A. POE.

Her Mother's Darling. By Mrs. J. H. RIDDELL.

Gaslight and Daylight. By GEORGE AUGUSTUS SALA.

Bound to the Wheel. By JOHN SAUNDERS.

Guy Waterman. J. SAUNDERS.

One Against the World. By JOHN SAUNDERS.

The Lion in the Path. By JOHN and KATHERINE SAUNDERS.

Match in the Dark. By A. SKETCHLEY.

Tales for the Marines. By WALTER THORNBURY.

The Way we Live Now. By ANTHONY TROLLOPE.

The American Senator. By ANTHONY TROLLOPE.

Diamond Cut Diamond. By T. A. TROLLOPE.

A Pleasure Trip on the Continent of Europe. By MARK TWAIN.

Adventures of Tom Sawyer. By MARK TWAIN.

An Idle Excursion. By MARK TWAIN.

Fcap. 8vo, picture covers, 1s. each.

Jeff Briggs's Love Story. By BRET HARTE.
The Twins of Table Mountain. By BRET HARTE.
Mrs. Gainsborough's Diamonds. By JULIAN HAWTHORNE.
Kathleen Mavourneen. By the Author of "That Lass o' Lowrie's."
Lindsay's Luck. By the Author of "That Lass o' Lowrie's."
Pretty Polly Pemberton. By Author of "That Lass o' Lowrie's."
Trooping with Crows. By Mrs. PIRKIS.
The Professor's Wife. By LEONARD GRAHAM.

Large 4to, cloth extra, gilt, beautifully Illustrated, 31*s.* 6*d.*

Pastoral Days ;

Or, Memories of a New England Year. By W. HAMILTON GIBSON.
With 76 Illustrations in the highest style of Wood Engraving.

"The volume contains a prose poem, with illustrations in the shape of wood engravings more beautiful than it can well enter into the hearts of most men to conceive. Mr. Gibson is not only the author of the text, he is the designer of the illustrations: and it would be difficult to say in which capacity he shows most of the true poet. There is a sensuous beauty in his prose which charms and lulls you. . . . But, as the illustrations are turned to, it will be felt that a new pleasure has been found. It would be difficult to express too high admiration of the exquisite delicacy of most of the engravings. They are proofs at once of Mr. Gibson's power as an artist, of the skill of the engravers, and of the marvellous excellence of the printer's work."—SCOTSMAN.

Crown 8vo, cloth extra, 6*s.*

Planche—Songs and Poems, from 1819 to 1879.

By J. R. PLANCHE. Edited, with an Introduction, by his Daughter, Mrs. MACKARNESS.

Two Vols. 8vo, cloth extra, with Illustrations, 10*s.* 6*d.*

Plutarch's Lives of Illustrious Men.

Translated from the Greek, with Notes, Critical and Historical, and a Life of Plutarch, by JOHN and WILLIAM LANGHORNE. New Edition, with Medallion Portraits.

Crown 8vo, cloth extra, 7*s.* 6*d.*

Primitive Manners and Customs.

By JAMES A. FARRER.

Small 8vo, cloth extra, with Illustrations, 3*s.* 6*d.*

Prince of Argolis, The:

A Story of the Old Greek Fairy Time. By J. MOYR SMITH. With 130 Illustrations by the Author.

Proctor's (R. A.) Works:

Easy Star Lessons for Young Learners. With Star Maps for Every Night in the Year, Drawings of the Constellations, &c. By RICHARD A. PROCTOR. Crown 8vo, cloth extra, 6*s.*   [*In preparation.*

Myths and Marvels of Astronomy. By RICH. A. PROCTOR, Author of "Other Worlds than Ours," &c. Crown 8vo, cloth extra, 6*s.*

Pleasant Ways in Science. By R. A. PROCTOR. Cr. 8vo, cl. ex. 6*s.*

Rough Ways made Smooth: A Series of Familiar Essays on Scientific Subjects. By R. A. PROCTOR. Crown 8vo, cloth extra, 6*s.*

Our Place among Infinities: A Series of Essays contrasting our Little Abode in Space and Time with the Infinities Around us. By RICHARD A. PROCTOR. Crown 8vo, cloth extra, 6*s.*

The Expanse of Heaven: A Series of Essays on the Wonders of the Firmament. By RICHARD A. PROCTOR. Crown 8vo, cloth, 6*s.*

Wages and Wants of Science Workers. By RICHARD A. PROCTOR. Crown 8vo, 1*s.* 6*d.*

"Mr. Proctor, of all writers of our time, best conforms to Matthew Arnold's conception of a man of culture, in that he strives to humanise knowledge, to divest it of whatever is harsh, crude, or technical, and so makes it a source of happiness and brightness for all."—WESTMINSTER REVIEW.

Crown 8vo, cloth extra, gilt, 7s. 6d.

Pursuivant of Arms, The;

or, Heraldry founded upon Facts. A Popular Guide to the Science of Heraldry. By J. R. PLANCHE, Somerset Herald. With Coloured Frontispiece, Plates, and 200 Illustrations.

Crown 8vo, cloth extra, with Illustrations, 7s. 6d.

Rabelais' Works.

Faithfully Translated from the French, with variorum Notes, and numerous characteristic Illustrations by GUSTAVE DORE.

Crown 8vo, cloth gilt, with numerous Illustrations, and a beautifully executed Chart of the various Spectra, 7s. 6d.

Rambosson's Astronomy.

By J. RAMBOSSON, Laureate of the Institute of France. Translated by C. B. PITMAN. Profusely Illustrated.

Second Edition, Revised, Crown 8vo, 1,200 pages, half-roxburghe, 12s. 6d.

Reader's Handbook (The) of Allusions, Re-

ferences, Plots, and Stories. By the Rev. Dr. Brewer.

"Dr. Brewer has produced a wonderfully comprehensive dictionary of references to matters which are always cropping up in conversation and in everyday life, and writers generally have reason to feel grateful to the author for a most handy volume, supplementing in a hundred ways their own knowledge or ignorance, as the case may be. . . . It is something more than a mere dictionary of quotations, though a most useful companion to any work of that kind, being a dictionary of most of the allusions, references, plots, stories, and characters which occur in the classical poems, plays, novels, romances, &c., not only of our own country, but of most nations, ancient and modern."—TIMES.

Crown 8vo, cloth extra, 6s.

Richardson's (Dr.) A Ministry of Health,

and other Papers. By BENJAMIN WARD RICHARDSON, M.D., &c.

Square 8vo, cloth extra, gilt, profusely Illustrated, 10s. 6d.

Rimmer's Our Old Country Towns.

With over 50 Illustrations. By ALFRED RIMMER.

Two Vols., large 4to, profusely Illustrated, half-morocco, £2 16s.

Rowlandson, the Caricaturist.

A Selection from his Works, with Anecdotal Descriptions of his Famous Caricatures, and a Sketch of his Life, Times, and Contemporaries. With nearly 400 Illustrations, mostly in Facsimile of the Originals. By JOSEPH GREGO, Author of "James Gillray, the Caricaturist; his Life, Works, and Times."

"Mr. Grego's excellent account of the works of Thomas Rowlandson . . . illustrated with some 400 spirited, accurate, and clever transcripts from his designs. . . . The thanks of all who care for what is original and personal in art are due to Mr. Grego for the pains he has been at, and the time he has expended, in the preparation of this very pleasant, very careful, and adequate memorial."—PALL MALL GAZETTE.

Handsomely printed, price 5s.

Roll of Battle Abbey, The;

or, A List of the Principal Warriors who came over from Normandy
with William the Conqueror, and Settled in this Country, A.D. 1066-7.
Printed on fine plate paper, nearly three feet by two, with the principal Arms emblazoned in Gold and Colours.

Crown 8vo, cloth extra, profusely Illustrated, 4s. 6d. each.

" Secret Out " Series, The.

The Pyrotechnist's Treasury;
or, Complete Art of Making Fire-
works. By THOMAS KENTISH. With
numerous Illustrations.

The Art of Amusing :
A Collection of Graceful Arts, Games,
Tricks, Puzzles, and Charades. By
FRANK BELLEW. 300 Illustrations.

Hanky-Panky :
Very Easy Tricks, Very Difficult
Tricks, White Magic, Sleight of Hand.
Edited by W.H. CREMER. 200 Illusts.

The Merry Circle :
A Book of New Intellectual Games
and Amusements. By CLARA BELLEW.
Many Illustrations.

Magician's Own Book :
Performances with Cups and Balls,
Eggs, Hats, Handkerchiefs, &c. All
from Actual Experience. Edited by
W. H. CREMER. 200 Illustrations.

Magic No Mystery :
Tricks with Cards, Dice, Balls, &c.,
with fully descriptive Directions ; the
Art of Secret Writing ; Training of
Performing Animals, &c. Coloured
Frontispiece and many Illustrations.

The Secret Out :
One Thousand Tricks with Cards, and
other Recreations ; with Entertaining
Experiments in Drawing-room or
" White Magic." By W. H. CREMER.
300 Engravings.

Crown 8vo, cloth extra, 6s.

Senior's Travel and Trout in the Antipodes.

An Angler's Sketches in Tasmania and New Zealand. By WILLIAM
SENIOR ("Red Spinner"), Author of "Stream and Sea."

Crown 8vo, cloth extra, gilt, with 10 full-page Tinted Illustrations, 7s. 6d.

Sheridan's Complete Works,

with Life and Anecdotes. Including his Dramatic Writings, printed
from the Original Editions, his Works in Prose and Poetry, Translations, Speeches, Jokes. Puns &c. ; with a Collection of Sheridaniana.

Crown 8vo, cloth extra, with Illustrations, 7s. 6d.

Signboards:

Their History. With Anecdotes of Famous Taverns and Remarkable
Characters. By JACOB LARWOOD and JOHN CAMDEN HOTTEN.
With nearly 100 Illustrations.

"*Even if we were ever so maliciously inclined, we could not pick out all Messrs.
Larwood and Hotten's plums, because the good things are so numerous as to defy
the most wholesale depredation.*"—TIMES.

Crown 8vo, cloth extra, gilt, 6s. 6d.

Slang Dictionary, The :

Etymological, Historical, and Anecdotal. An ENTIRELY NEW
EDITION, revised throughout, and considerably Enlarged.

"*We are glad to see the Slang Dictionary reprinted and enlarged. From a high
scientific point of view this book is not to be despised. Of course it cannot fail to
be amusing also. It contains the very vocabula.y of unrestrained humour, and
oddity, and grotesqueness. In a word, it provides valuable material both for the
student of language and the student of human nature.*"—ACADEMY.

Shakespeare:

Shakespeare, The First Folio. Mr. WILLIAM SHAKESPEARE'S Comedies, Histories, and Tragedies. Published according to the true Originall Copies. London, Printed by ISAAC IAGGARD and ED. BLOUNT, 1623.—A Reproduction of the extremely rare original, in reduced facsimile by a photographic process—ensuring the strictest accuracy in every detail. Small 8vo, half-Roxburghe, 7s. 6d.

*" To Messrs. Chatto and Windus belongs the merit of having done more to facilitate the critical study of the text of our great dramatist than all the Shakespeare clubs and societies put together. A complete facsimile of the celebrated First Folio edition of 1623 for half-a-guinea is at once a miracle of cheapness and enterprise. Being in a reduced form, the type is necessarily rather diminutive, but it is as distinct as in a genuine copy of the original, and will be found to be as useful and far more handy to the student than the latter."—*ATHENÆUM.

Shakespeare, The Lansdowne. Beautifully printed in red and black, in small but very clear type. With engraved facsimile of DROESHOUT's Portrait. Post 8vo, cloth extra, 7s. 6d.

Shakespeare for Children: Tales from Shakespeare. By CHARLES and MARY LAMB. With numerous Illustrations, coloured and plain, by J. MOYR SMITH. Crown 4to, cloth gilt, 10s. 6d.

Shakespeare Music, The Handbook of. Being an Account of 350 Pieces of Music, set to Words taken from the Plays and Poems of Shakespeare, the compositions ranging from the Elizabethan Age to the Present Time. By ALFRED ROFFE. 4to, half-Roxburghe, 7s.

Shakespeare, A Study of. By ALGERNON CHARLES SWIN-BURNE. Crown 8vo, cloth extra, 8s.

Exquisitely printed in miniature, cloth extra, gilt edges, 2s. 6d.

Smoker's Text-Book, The.
By J. HAMER, F.R.S.L.

Crown 8vo, cloth extra, 5s.

Spalding's Elizabethan Demonology:
An Essay in Illustration of the Belief in the Existence of Devils, and the Powers possessed by them. By T. ALFRED SPALDING, LL.B.

Crown 4to, uniform with "Chaucer for Children," with Coloured Illustrations, cloth gilt, 10s. 6d.

Spenser for Children.
By M. H. TOWRY. With Illustrations in Colours by WALTER J. MORGAN.

"Spenser has simply been transferred into plain prose, with here and there a line or stanza quoted, where the meaning and the diction are within a child's comprehension, and additional point is thus given to the narrative without the cost of obscurity. . . . Altogether the work has been well and carefully done."—THE TIMES.

Crown 8vo, cloth extra, 9s.

Stedman's Victorian Poets:
Critical Essays. By EDMUND CLARENCE STEDMAN.

" We ought to be thankful to those who do critical work with competent skill and understanding. Mr. Stedman deserves the thanks of English scholars; . . . he is faithful, studious, and discerning."—SATURDAY REVIEW.

Post 8vo, cloth extra, 5s.

Stories about Number Nip,

The Spirit of the Giant Mountains. Retold for Children, by WALTER
GRAHAME. With Illustrations by J. MOYR SMITH.

Crown 8vo, with a Map of Suburban London, cloth extra, 7s. 6d.

Suburban Homes (The) of London:

A Residential Guide to Favourite London Localities, their Society,
Celebrities, and Associations. With Notes on their Rental, Rates,
and House Accommodation.

Crown 8vo, cloth extra, with Illustrations, 7s. 6d.

Swift's Choice Works,

In Prose and Verse. With Memoir, Portrait, and Facsimiles of the
Maps in the Original Edition of "Gulliver's Travels."

Demy 8vo, cloth extra, Illustrated, 21s.

Sword, The Book of the:

Being a History of the Sword, and its Use, in all Times and in all
Countries. By Captain RICHARD BURTON. With numerous Illustrations.   [*In preparation.*

Crown 8vo, cloth extra, with Illustrations, 7s. 6d.

Strutt's Sports and Pastimes of the People

of England; including the Rural and Domestic Recreations, May
Games, Mummeries, Shows, Processions, Pageants, and Pompous
Spectacles, from the Earliest Period to the Present Time. With 140
Illustrations. Edited by WILLIAM HONE.

Swinburne's Works:

The Queen Mother and Rosa-
mond. Fcap. 8vo, 5s.

Atalanta in Calydon.
A New Edition. Crown 8vo, 6s.

Chastelard.
A Tragedy. Crown 8vo, 7s.

Poems and Ballads.
FIRST SERIES. Fcap. 8vo, 9s. Also
in crown 8vo, at same price.

Poems and Ballads.
SECOND SERIES. Fcap. 8vo, 9s. Also
in crown 8vo, at same price.

Notes on "Poems and Bal-
lads." 8vo, 1s.

William Blake:
A Critical Essay. With Facsimile
Paintings. Demy 8vo, 16s.

Songs before Sunrise.
Crown 8vo, 10s. 6d.

Bothwell:
A Tragedy. Crown 8vo, 12s. 6d.

George Chapman:
An Essay. Crown 8vo, 7s.

Songs of Two Nations.
Crown 8vo, 6s.

Essays and Studies.
Crown 8vo, 12s.

Erechtheus:
A Tragedy. Crown 8vo, 6s.

Note of an English Republican
on the Muscovite Crusade. 8vo, 1s.

A Note on Charlotte Brontë.
Crown 8vo, 6s.

A Study of Shakespeare.
Crown 8vo, 8s.

Songs of the Springtides. Cr.
8vo, 6s.

Studies in Song.
Crown 8vo, 7s.

Medium 8vo, cloth extra, with Illustrations, 7s. 6d.

Syntax's (Dr.) Three Tours,

in Search of the Picturesque, in Search of Consolation, and in Search of a Wife. With the whole of ROWLANDSON'S droll page Illustrations, in Colours, and Life of the Author by J. C. HOTTEN.

Crown 8vo, cloth gilt, profusely Illustrated, 6s.

Tales of Old Thule.

Collected and Illustrated by J. MOYR SMITH.

Four Vols. small 8vo, cloth boards, 30s.

Taine's History of English Literature.

Translated by HENRY VAN LAUN.

. Also a POPULAR EDITION, in Two Vols. crown 8vo, cloth extra, 15s.

One Vol. crown 8vo, cloth extra, 7s. 6d.

Taylor's (Tom) Historical Dramas:

"Clancarty," "Jeanne Darc," "'Twixt Axe and Crown," "The Fool's Revenge," "Arkwright's Wife," "Anne Boleyn," "Plot and Passion."

. The Plays may also be had separately, at 1s. each.

Crown 8vo, cloth extra, with Coloured Frontispiece and numerous Illustrations, 7s. 6d.

Thackerayana:

Notes and Anecdotes. Illustrated by a profusion of Sketches by WILLIAM MAKEPEACE THACKERAY, depicting Humorous Incidents in his School-life, and Favourite Characters in the books of his every-day reading. With Hundreds of Wood Engravings, facsimiled from Mr. Thackeray's Original Drawings.

Crown 8vo, cloth extra, gilt edges, with Illustrations, 7s. 6d.

Thomson's Seasons and Castle of Indolence.

With a Biographical and Critical Introduction by ALLAN CUNNINGHAM, and over 50 fine Illustrations on Steel and Wood.

Crown 8vo, cloth extra, with numerous Illustrations, 7s. 6d.

Thornbury's (Walter) Haunted London.

A New Edition, Edited by EDWARD WALFORD, M.A., with numerous Illustrations by F. W. FAIRHOLT, F.S.A.

"Mr. Thornbury knew and loved his London. . . . He had read much history, and every by-lane and every court had associations for him. His memory and his note-books were stored with anecdote, and, as he had singular skill in the matter of narration it will be readily believed that when he took to writing a set book about the places he knew and cared for, the said book would be charming. Charming the volume before us certainly is. It may be begun in the beginning, or middle, or end, it is all one: wherever one lights, there is some pleasant and curious bit of gossip, some amusing fragment of allusion or quotation."—VANITY FAIR.

Crown 8vo, cloth extra, with Illustrations, 7s. 6d.

Timbs' Clubs and Club Life in London.

With Anecdotes of its famous Coffee-houses, Hostelries, and Taverns. By JOHN TIMBS, F.S.A. With numerous Illustrations.

Crown 8vo, cloth extra, with Illustrations, 7s. 6d.

Timbs' English Eccentrics and Eccentrici-

ties: Stories of Wealth and Fashion, Delusions, Impostures, and Fanatic Missions, Strange Sights and Sporting Scenes, Eccentric Artists, Theatrical Folks, Men of Letters, &c. By JOHN TIMBS, F.S.A. With nearly 50 Illustrations.

Demy 8vo, cloth extra, 14s.

Torrens' The Marquess Wellesley,

Architect of Empire. An Historic Portrait. *Forming Vol. I. of* PRO-CONSUL and TRIBUNE: WELLESLEY and O'CONNELL: Historic Portraits. By W. M. TORRENS, M.P. In Two Vols.

Crown 8vo, cloth extra, with Coloured Illustrations, 7s. 6d.

Turner's (J. M. W.) Life and Correspondence:

Founded upon Letters and Papers furnished by his Friends and fellow-Academicians. By WALTER THORNBURY. A New Edition, considerably Enlarged. With numerous Illustrations in Colours, facsimiled from Turner's original Drawings.

Two Vols., crown 8vo, cloth extra, with Map and Ground-Plans, 14s.

Walcott's Church Work and Life in English

Minsters; and the English Student's Monasticon. By the Rev. MACKENZIE E. C. WALCOTT, B.D.

The Twenty-first Annual Edition, for 1881, cloth, full gilt, 50s.

Walford's County Families of the United

Kingdom. A Royal Manual of the Titled and Untitled Aristocracy of Great Britain and Ireland. By EDWARD WALFORD, M.A., late Scholar of Balliol College, Oxford. Containing Notices of the Descent, Birth, Marriage, Education, &c., of more than 12,000 distinguished Heads of Families in the United Kingdom, their Heirs Apparent or Presumptive, together with a Record of the Patronage at their disposal, the Offices which they hold or have held, their Town Addresses, Country Residences, Clubs, &c.

Large crown 8vo, cloth antique, with Illustrations, 7s. 6d.

Walton and Cotton's Complete Angler;

or, The Contemplative Man's Recreation : being a Discourse of Rivers. Fishponds, Fish and Fishing, written by IZAAK WALTON; and Instructions how to Angle for a Trout or Grayling in a clear Stream, by CHARLES COTTON. With Original Memoirs and Notes by Sir HARRIS NICOLAS, and 61 Copperplate Illustrations.

Carefully printed on paper to imitate the Original, 22 in. by 14 in., 2s.

Warrant to Execute Charles I.

An exact Facsimile of this important Document, with the Fifty-nine Signatures of the Regicides, and corresponding Seals.

Beautifully printed on paper to imitate the Original MS., price 2s.

Warrant to Execute Mary Queen of Scots.
An exact Facsimile, including the Signature of Queen Elizabeth, and a Facsimile of the Great Seal.

Crown 8vo, cloth limp, with numerous Illustrations, 4s. 6d.

Westropp's Handbook of Pottery and Porce-
lain ; or, History of those Arts from the Earliest Period. By HODDER M. WESTROPP, Author of " Handbook of Archæology," &c. With numerous beautiful Illustrations, and a List of Marks.

SEVENTH EDITION. Square 8vo, 1s.

Whistler v. Ruskin: Art and Art Critics.
By J. A. MACNEILL WHISTLER.

Crown 8vo, cloth limp, with Illustrations, 2s. 6d.

Williams' A Simple Treatise on Heat.
By W. MATTIEU WILLIAMS, F.R.A.S., F.C.S.

" *This is an unpretending little work, put forth for the purpose of expounding in simple style the phenomena and laws of heat. No strength is vainly spent in endeavouring to present a mathematical view of the subject. The author passes over the ordinary range of matter to be found in most elementary treatises on heat, and enlarges upon the applications of the principles of his science—a subject which is naturally attractive to the uninitiated. Mr. Williams's object has been well carried out, and his little book may be recommended to those who care to study this interesting branch of physics.*"—POPULAR SCIENCE REVIEW.

A HANDSOME GIFT-BOOK.— Small 8vo, cloth extra, 6s.

Wooing (The) of the Water-Witch:
A Northern Oddity. By EVAN DALDORNE. With One Hundred and Twenty-five fine Illustrations by J. MOYR SMITH.

Crown 8vo, half-bound, 12s. 6d.

Words and Phrases:
A Dictionary of Curious, Quaint, and Out-of-the-Way Matters. By ELIEZER EDWARDS. [*In the press.*

Crown 8vo, cloth extra, with Illustrations, 7s. 6d.

Wright's Caricature History of the Georges.
(The House of Hanover.) With 400 Pictures, Caricatures, Squibs, Broadsides, Window Pictures, &c. By THOMAS WRIGHT, M.A., F.S.A.

Large post 8vo, cloth extra, gilt, with Illustrations, 7s. 6d.

Wright's History of Caricature and of the
Grotesque in Art, Literature, Sculpture, and Painting, from the Earliest Times to the Present Day. By THOMAS WRIGHT, M.A., F.S.A. Profusely Illustrated by F. W. FAIRHOLT, F.S.A.

J. OGDEN AND CO., PRINTERS, 172, ST. JOHN STREET, E.C.

www.ingramcontent.com/pod-product-compliance
Lightning Source LLC
Chambersburg PA
CBHW020853020726
47497CB00005B/1386